"Who broke it off?"

He did not just ask that, did he? As if it was his business? Because it wasn't. Remembering the price tag on this gig made her play nice when she longed to tell Drew Slade to mind his own business. She couldn't do that so she shrugged lightly. "He did."

Drew studied her for long, thick seconds, long enough for her heart to do that step-toe dance again. Then he leaned closer. "He's a moron, Kimber, but I might just send him a thank-you note."

Kimberly was pretty sure her breathing paused as their eyes met. "What for?"

He winked.

Her heart stuttered. Because Drew Slade had just flirted with her. Sure, he was just trying to ease an awkward moment, but that one brief exchange was enough to stir up those old schoolgirl feelings.

But that was then and this was now, and a whole lot of ugly had passed under their respective bridges.

Multipublished, bestselling author **Ruth Logan Herne** loves God, her country, her family, dogs, chocolate and coffee! Married to a very patient man, she lives in an old farmhouse in upstate New York and thinks possums should leave the cat food alone and snakes should always live outside. There are no exceptions to either rule! Visit Ruthy at ruthloganherne.com.

Books by Ruth Logan Herne

Love Inspired

Grace Haven

An Unexpected Groom

Kirkwood Lake

The Lawman's Second Chance
Falling for the Lawman
The Lawman's Holiday Wish
Loving the Lawman
Her Holiday Family
Healing the Lawman's Heart

Men of Allegany County

Reunited Hearts
Small-Town Hearts
Mended Hearts
Yuletide Hearts
A Family to Cherish
His Mistletoe Family

Big Sky Centennial

His Montana Sweetheart

Visit the Author Profile page at Harlequin.com for more titles.

An Unexpected Groom

Ruth Logan Herne

Recycling programs for this product may not exist in your area.

ISBN-13: 978-0-373-81884-6

An Unexpected Groom

This edition published by arrangement with Love Inspired Books.

www.Harlequin.com

Printed in U.S.A.

Be kind to one another, tenderhearted,
forgiving one another, as God in Christ forgave you.
—*Ephesians* 4:32

This book is dedicated to the family of NYS Trooper Andrew "A.J." Sperr, a fine young man from my church who lost his life in the line of duty in 2006 while serving as a NYS State Trooper. May God bless his family and his fellow officers who still mourn A.J.'s loss daily. A memorial has been erected in Big Flats, NY, to commemorate A.J.'s life and service. The website for Sperr Memorial Park is sperrmemorialpark.org.

Acknowledgments

I actually got paid to research this book!

For eight years I was blessed to work as a bridal consultant in a wonderful store, Bridal Hall, in Rochester, New York, run by the Hall family. The Hall family taught me the ins and outs of wedding planning, bridal sales, organizing wedding parties, alterations and teaching me to be that friendly listener, so crucial to happy weddings! They then went on to employ two of my kids as they attended the University of Rochester on the "tuxedo" side of the store, renting out men's formal wear and booking groom's parties. On slow winter nights, my boss encouraged Beth and then Luke to bring their university books to study as needed. Their strong family ties and the way they embraced so many of their employees and customers was a first-class example of small business at its finest. I'm proud to acknowledge them in this book.

Also huge thanks to my local police departments. I am honored to include several local police officers/ sheriffs among my friends and they deserve a public shout-out for their ongoing dedication and service. May God bless them heartily and keep them from harm.

Chapter One

It's not that you can do this, Kimberly Gallagher's conscience prodded as she strode through the elegantly appointed welcoming area of her mother's central New York wedding and event-organizing enterprise. *It's that you must do it. And you hate having someone else call the shots.* Although having other people call the shots had been her new status update the past few months.

She'd been dumped by a fiancé, had been let go from a job she excelled at and her father's grim diagnosis of brain cancer had stripped Kimberly of the notion that she was in charge.

She walked into her mother's office and took a seat to prepare for her only appointment of the day. She was about to meet with the chief security officer for the upcoming pricey wedding of Senator Rick Vandeveld's oldest daughter. Shelby had organized her special day with Kimberly's mother months ago. Now they should be able to tweak minor details and put the plan in motion.

Simple, really.

A photo of her parents sat centered on her mother's desk. Her mother smiled at the camera in typical friendly fashion. Her police chief father ignored the camera and smiled down at his wife, showing his priorities clearly. He didn't care what others thought.

He cared about his wife.

Staid and solid, in the daily uniform he wore with pride, her father had dedicated decades to the Grace Haven force, an honest cop that bled New York blue even after losing his only son to the uniform more than ten years ago. Pete Gallagher was in the fight of his life right now, with his wife by his side, and anything Kimberly and her sisters could do to make that easier was an honor.

If they didn't kill one another first.

A soft melodic chime said her appointment had just walked into the reception area.

Dread poked Kimberly's midsection. It wasn't the logistics of working Shelby's wedding that bothered her. It was the fairy-tale headline of Future President's Daughter Weds Country Star, when Kimberly should have been planning *her* own wedding, *her* reception, *her* happy-ever-after.

That had turned into an epic fail, so today she was handling someone else's shot at the gold ring. A bride, a groom, a hillside vineyard, a grotto and a sprawling palatial inn overlooking the beauty of Canandaigua Lake.

Envy snaked a cool thread up her spine.

She forced it down and stood as Allison, her mother's senior assistant, opened the door. Kimberly rounded the desk, turned and came face-to-face with the last person she expected to see back in the Finger Lakes region of upstate New York. The guy who'd lost a partner—*her brother*—in a sting operation gone bad more than a decade ago.

He stared at her, and the majestic German shepherd walking at his side stared, too.

She stopped, her eyes glued to his, wondering how this could have happened. Hazel eyes, more somber than they used to be. Dark hair, wavy, cut short. Tall enough to make her look up, even in three-inch heels. Her heart went silent. The tips of her fingers buzzed. And if respiration was governed by an autonomous system, why couldn't she draw a breath?

Andrew Slade breathed first. "When I spoke with your mother on the phone a few weeks ago, you were a bigwig events planner for a successful Nashville record label. What are you doing here?"

A simple enough question to answer in the middle of a convoluted moment. She inhaled, then exhaled to calm her nerves. "Financial restructuring meant downsizing."

"They fired you?"

He had the nerve to look indignant, as if what happened to others mattered to him. Kimberly knew better. "They're on a temporary barebones budget, but yes." She kept her gaze cool despite the fact that his look of indignation felt good. She'd worked long and hard at STAC Records, a hot country label that had hit the wall mid-June. The firm's plan was to hire her back once they'd resolved the books, but in the meantime she was here, facing a man who'd stirred her heart and then her anger many years ago.

"Although the timing is good." Drew glanced around the office, then at her mother's chair. "Listen, Kimber, I know this is awkward."

Nailed it!

"And I'm the last person you expected to see walk through the door."

Two for two, the guy is on a roll.

He put an easy hand on the dog's head. "If you'd rather have Emily handle this, I understand completely."

Her younger sister Emily take charge of a

top-tier event like this? Talk about a free fall into catastrophe. "You can't be serious."

His expression said he was quite serious. None of the old laugh lines she knew—and liked so well when she was a love-struck teen, crushing on the guy before her—were in evidence now.

"There's no way that Em—"

Fury erupted beyond the door.

Drew turned, instantly on guard. So did his dog, hackles raised, shoulders up, head strained.

Mags, her mother's eight-pound Yorkshire terrier, launched into her yipping and yapping, the normally well-behaved pooch streaked across the reception room carpet, feet and fur flying, and when she crested Kate's glassed-in office door, she braced her front paws, bared her teeth and gave a fairly convincing growl, as if the difference in height, weight, training and attitude between her and the impressive K-9 wasn't ridiculously obvious.

"Mags!" Kimberly's sister Emily chased after the dog. "You bad puppy, this is what we get because Mom spoiled you." She reached down, picked up the dust-mop dog, then stood. "Drew?" She stepped forward to greet their childhood friend, then gave a dramatic pause, gaze pinned to the bigger dog between them. "Will he eat me? Or her?" She angled a look to the little dog in her arms. The Yorkie rewarded her with quick kisses to the cheek.

"Her, possibly." Drew looked at Mags. "You? Only if I issue the command, and I'm feeling altruistic today. We've declared beauty queens to be non–life threatening in most instances."

"Former beauty queen," she reminded him, and then gave him a hug. "It's nice to have you home, Drew."

Kimberly's heart tightened.

So did Drew's face. "It's where the job brought me. I was just telling Kimberly that if you'd rather handle Shelby's wedding, we'd be fine with that."

Emily's look of fear was only half in jest. "Not in this lifetime. Kimberly gets lead on this, totally. I don't mind helping out with things, but I'm the schmoozer of the family. When Kimberly steps on toes…"

Kimberly tapped a toe on the floor, unamused.

The toe-tap did nothing to deter the middle Gallagher sister. "I jump in to smooth ruffled feathers, but major events like a presidential candidate's daughter marrying a country star?" She put her free hand up, palm out. "Out of my league. Kimber takes lead on Shelby's event while I'm helping her handle the fall regatta, three weddings, several bridal and baby showers, two corporate dinners and a fall festival dinner dance. I consider that a fair trade."

Kimberly would trade off in a heartbeat if she could, but Emily was right. She'd commanded top dollar in Nashville for putting together major events. To thrust that on Emily would be unfair to her and probably spell disaster for the Vandeveld wedding.

Emily backed toward the door with the Yorkie. "I'm taking Mags upstairs with me so that...?" She raised a brow, silently asking the shepherd's name.

"Rocky."

"So Rocky can go the rounds with you guys undisturbed. He's beautiful, Drew."

"Thank you."

The door swung noiselessly shut behind her.

"Well."

"Well." He took a seat as Kimberly rounded the desk to her mother's chair. She opened the portfolio and started to withdraw her mother's notes. Drew laid one big, strong hand on the portfolio and shook his head.

She raised her eyes, confused. "You don't want to see the plans?"

"No need because we're going to change the plans," he told her, "which means Shelby will most likely hate me. I'm willing to risk it to keep her and her guitar-picking husband and their guests alive."

"Change the plans?" Kimberly indicated the desktop calendar in front of her, dumbfounded. "The wedding is two months away. You can't—"

"Can, will and must." He moved his hand, but he didn't relax into the chair like most people would. He sat, back straight, shoulders squared, head high, on alert. "Rick Vandeveld is most likely going to be our president-elect in nine short weeks. The reason I couldn't make the original planning meeting with your mother was because threats against him on the campaign trail kept me tied up. An open affair like Shelby planned?" He shook his head. "Indefensible. The stakes changed the minute Rick actually became the party candidate. That means we start again. From the beginning."

He couldn't be serious. The Finger Lakes had become a go-to destination for weddings and events. Changing a date on a huge affair like this would be impossible. "Do you have the authority to change it?" she squeaked the words in disbelief, because this couldn't get worse.

Kimberly had organized major galas for stars and corporate bigwigs in Nashville, but she'd cut her event-planning teeth in her mother's primarily bridal business. Crossing a bride was never in anyone's best interests. But what would a single guy like Drew Slade know about that? Nothing. "Look, Andrew."

He didn't wince when she used his whole name. She'd wanted him to; she wanted him to know she wasn't letting bygones be bygones. Their childhood familiarity had dissolved when her brother lay bleeding on a cold, wet asphalt parking lot a decade ago because Drew had pulled into the sting a few minutes late. The first rule of police work was "cover your partner's back."

Drew failed and Dave died.

He met her gaze, cool, calm and collected, totally take-charge, but this wasn't realigning a parade route for visibility's sake.

This was a wedding. The senator's daughter's wedding. One of the most important days in a woman's life, so Drew could—

"I not only have the authority—I have the final say. Nothing about this wedding gets done without my approval. There are no ad-libs. There are no unapproved breaks in the itinerary. There are no unexpected last-minute changes."

Drew Slade needed a major reality check. "Those things are a given in a wedding."

"Not this time." He nodded toward the portfolio her mother and Shelby had threaded together several months before. "Everything gets handled differently now that Rick is the party's candidate. Shelby's a politician's daughter. She'll understand."

He was half-right.

As a politician's daughter, Shelby would understand the need to prioritize safety. Kimberly had organized tight security at numerous Nashville events. The merging of a country star with a senator's daughter warranted security to the max with just the guest list, not to mention the main-event players.

But no bride on earth would hand over carte blanche control of her wedding day to a security employee, no matter how amazingly handsome, rugged and wounded he was. "Andrew, I appreciate your stand, but I really can't make any changes in Shelby's wedding itinerary without her permission."

He withdrew a phone, hit a number and waited. Her rebuttal hadn't angered him, probably because he ran into security snags and unwilling people regularly in his job. But changing a wedding?

Not on her watch.

He handed her the phone. "Shelby would like to speak to you."

She reached out to take it.

Their eyes met. Their hands touched, and for fleeting seconds that one-sided high school crush barreled back, teenage emotions of falling for big brother's best friend. Andrew and Dave, always together. Childhood friends, high school teammates, college roomies and then cops together on the streets of Rochester. Until Dave was just…gone.

Focus on the phone.

She brought it to her ear and turned slightly away from Drew's intensity. "Shelby? It's Kimberly Gallagher from Kate & Company. How are you?"

"Exhausted, muddled and wishing my wedding day was a thing of the past, right along with this election. But that's off the record, Kimberly! In the press I'm smiling and pleased and delighted to be here, supporting my dad."

Kimberly knew the feeling well. "I hear you. So, listen, Andrew Slade is here and he's—"

"I know exactly what he's doing."

Kimberly's heart fell, because Shelby's droll tone spelled t-r-o-u-b-l-e without the acoustic guitar.

"And I don't know how you're going to deal with him, Kimberly. He's such an old bear when it comes to keeping us safe, but then again, that's why we hired him. Listen, he's going to fuss and bother, then he's going to think about it a while and then he'll devise a plan to make things work. Honestly, if Travis and I had thought things through, we'd have either waited or eloped, but my mother would be brokenhearted if I did that. And a girl can't go through life disappointing her mother."

Kimberly decided she liked Shelby Vandeveld from afar.

"So here's how I'd like to handle this."

Kimberly lifted a pencil to take notes.

"Give Drew whatever he needs. He's got the weight of the world on his shoulders, and as long as I show up there and marry my best friend, I'm good."

"You're serious?"

"Not as often as my daddy would like, but on this, yes. See what you can save, call me to let me know about changes, email me pictures. Oops, gotta go. Family photo op and cheese tasting! I just love Wisconsin!"

She hung up.

So did Kimberly. She turned slowly. "So that's Shelby."

"It is. And she extended her permission, I take it."

"She said we can rearrange as needed, to keep her informed and she needed to go taste some cheese."

He made a face of acceptance. "Life in the fast lane of vote grooming. So." He stood and kept his eyes on hers. "Shall we go see what she and your mother planned? And then we'll adjust as needed."

Kimberly bit back the scolding she longed to give. When the Finger Lakes became a go-to spot for weddings and events, her mother had created a business that flourished. The downside was there were few alternative sites at this late date. Every elegant winery, hotel, inn, church and lakeside view had been booked for months if not years. Picturesque autumn in the Finger Lakes drew crowds from all over.

She bit her tongue, stood, lifted the thin portfolio and moved to the door. "Let's go."

Beautiful, bright and still blaming him for Dave's death. If Drew could rewind the hands of time, he'd have fixed that dreadful night, hundreds of times.

God's timing. Not yours.

He knew that. He'd finally come to accept it. But seeing the hollowness in Kimber's gaze when she looked at him brought the loss rushing back.

And now they'd be working side by side on a wedding that couldn't have been more poorly timed. He followed her through the door, trying not to notice how gracefully she moved. The fitted sundress made that an impossible task and her long blond hair shifted with each step forward.

He shifted his gaze to the floor. Spiky bright yellow heels thwarted that strategy.

Just admit it. She's gorgeous. She hates you. You've got no choice but to work together. You're doomed.

Rocky paused. Barked. Then barked again.

"Kimberly, hold up." Drew put his hand over the ever-present weapon at his hip.

She stopped and turned. "Because?"

He shook his head. "I'm not sure. Stay here." He ignored the impatient look she shot to the receptionist as he studied the layout.

Rocky barked again, but he didn't aim forward, toward the entrance facing the town square. He turned right, then left as if zeroing in, then moved toward the back of the offices. "What's down that hall?"

"Restrooms and the back door to the parking lot."

"Is it unlocked?"

Kimberly nodded. "Of course."

He frowned, but they'd talk about security changes later. Right now—

He gave Rocky a hand sign.

The broad-shouldered shepherd rushed down the hall, paused, then turned in a half circle. He whined softly, sat, then whined again, like he did when—

Drew stopped that train of thought instantly, because his beautiful eleven-year-old daughter was nearly six hours away at an exclusive Connecticut girls' camp, a gift from her maternal grandparents. She couldn't possibly be…

He turned the corner into the recessed alcove.

Amy Sue Slade looked up at him from a seat on the floor, and she had the nerve to smile. "Um… Hi."

"Hi?" He stared at his daughter, then the door, then her again. "Where did you come from, how did you get here and do you have any last wishes to make before I initiate your death sentence?"

She blanched and stood, but she didn't look nearly as worried as she should have when her life was on the line. "I told you I hated it there."

"Telling me you're unhappy and running away from camp are distinctively different things."

"It was literally like four turns to get from there to here, a straight shot across Interstate 90," she protested. "Connecticut and New York share a lot of latitude lines. Not even the least bit dangerous."

Kimberly came up alongside him, which meant this might not be the best moment for a family brawl. But eleven-year-olds should do what they were told. Always. "You took a train—"

"A bus, actually," she corrected him. "The nearest trains don't stop until Rochester and the cab ride back here would have wiped out my debit card."

"You got on a bus with who knows what kind of people and rode it here?"

"Yes."

"You are grounded forever."

"Okay."

"I mean it, Amy Sue. Forever."

"I know, Dad. You always mean everything you say." She let her backpack slide to the floor and held out her arms. "Did you miss me as much as I missed you?"

"More." He opened his arms. She fell into them, and the feel of holding his precious daughter tipped some of his world back on course. Rick's eighteen-month campaign had taken too big a toll on their time together. Once this election was done, so was he. He'd take his delightful daughter and find a quiet, cozy place to settle down and be the family they'd never had a chance to be. "Whose idea was it to send you to camp in the first place? What were we thinking, splitting up Team Slade?"

"It was Grandma's idea because you don't have time to watch me right now."

"And that hasn't changed one bit." He sighed, held her close, felt her tears and couldn't suppress the feeling that things just got a little more right in his world.

The back door swung open. Daryl Jackson, his security point man, strode in and smiled. "She found you."

"So it seems."

"I saw her edging around back."

"You could have radioed."

Daryl's grin flashed in his bronzed face. "More fun this way. So, Miss Amy, before he kills you dead, sweet thing, do you have a hug for me because now I'm going to have to listen to him complain about what to do with you while we're working. A hug is downright necessary in that case."

"Uncle Daryl!" She grinned and launched herself into Daryl's arms, then turned toward Kimberly.

Drew turned also. He wasn't sure what he expected to see on Kimberly's face, but compassion hadn't made the short list. "Kimberly."

She looked up and arched a brow that hinted amusement.

"Yes?"

He hauled in a breath and drew Amy forward. "My daughter, Amy Slade."

Kimberly squatted, and in that formfitting dress and three-inch heels, he was pretty sure squatting was no easy task. And then she smiled right at Amy, and that smile took him a long ways back. Emily might have been the beauty queen of the family, but in Drew's eyes, Kimberly had always been the beauty. And still was.

"You look just like your dad did when he was your age."

"For real?" Amy made a cute face and looked up. "No one's ever told me that before, but then I've never met anyone who knew Dad when he was young."

Kimberly graciously ignored the whys and wherefores of his hometown absence. "Now you have, and I assure you, you're a chip off the old block, and I'd venture to say that your little adventure today is the kind of thing your dad would have done."

Amy grasped his hand. "I don't like being away from Dad for even a little while. Three weeks was way too long, and then I was going to be shipped off to boarding school for the rest of the campaign. If I can't handle three weeks apart, I can't even think about months. That would be like the most awful, ever. And I'm not exactly like the other girls at the camp."

"Rich? Cultured? Well educated?" Drew listed the attributes in a wry voice.

She slanted her father a look that said he was being too generous. "I was going straight to unathletic, boring and pretentious, but we can add rich to the list. Now that doesn't matter." She hugged her father's arm, clearly delighted. "As long as I'm with Dad, everything's okay."

"Except it's not," Drew reminded her. "I'm working. Daryl's working. Your grandparents are touring Australia. We have to focus, Amy, and there's something about a daredevil kid hanging around that splits my attention. The perils of being a single dad," he added, for Kimberly's benefit.

"She can ride with us today, can't she?" Kimberly turned slightly. "And by the way, Daryl?" She reached across Amy to shake Daryl's hand. "I'm Kimberly."

"A pleasure, ma'am."

"You won't mind?" Drew asked. Shelby's wedding was a seriously priced six-figure deal, and having a kid ride along wasn't professional.

"Do you like to talk, Amy?" Kimberly looked down again.

The girl grinned. "Far too much, my dad says."

"Perfect." Kimberly moved toward the reception area. "An instant cure for grown-up awkward silence. She's absolutely welcome to come along."

"Sweet!" Amy squeezed his hand, grinning, before she hurried ahead to catch up with Kimberly.

This wasn't sweet, Drew decided. It was

uncomfortable and problematic, because as much as he loved his daughter, he was committed to making sure Shelby's wedding went off without a hitch. International terrorists and domestic unrest didn't allow a margin of error. His focus needed to be strictly on this upcoming event, but walking in front of him, side by side, were two reasons that wasn't going to happen, and he wasn't at all sure what to do about it.

He paused and called the camp to withdraw Amy's name from their registry and reassured the camp director that he didn't intend to sue. He put the necessary call to Eve's parents on hold. Explaining Amy's actions to them would take more time than he had right now. Their probable indignation over the lost funds would be completely understandable, and the time difference between Grace Haven and Adelaide iced the cake. Best to leave that until later.

He hung up the phone to rejoin the diverse group waiting for him. He'd have decisions to make soon, major ones, but right now strategizing this wedding took precedence. With Amy underfoot and Kimberly's tightly wound emotions, he wasn't sure how they were going to manage it, but if something went wrong at this beautiful, heartfelt affair, the guilt would fall on him. He'd left police work because of gut-wrenching guilt. It wasn't something he wanted to face, ever again.

Chapter Two

"This can be immediately scrapped from the list of possible venues," Drew told Kimberly as she directed him up the sloping drive of the rose-trellis-backed vineyard.

"It's a beautiful fall wedding venue," she argued. But from his point of view, she saw the problems immediately.

"Too open, too visible, one exit and entrance." Drew shook his head.

"It is her wedding day," Kimberly reminded him softly.

"And my goal is to get her to the honeymoon safely." His grim look drew worry lines in his forehead. The Drew she remembered didn't worry about anything, ever. Decisive and sure, he took everything in stride.

This Drew was different. "This is vulnerable. There's no way we can have the future president of the United States sitting here in the open with so many unprotected vantage points. The Secret Service would have a field day with this, Kimber." He used the childhood nickname as if they were still old friends. They weren't. So why did it sound so nice when he said it? That was something Kimberly would examine more closely later. Or not at all.

"If they swoop in and change everything last minute, we'll have wedding-day chaos. Let's avoid that, okay?"

A man moved up, out of the vineyard area, and started to approach the car.

Rocky went ballistic in the rear of the SUV. Front paws braced, barking and snarling. Kimberly's heart and nerves landed somewhere in the area of her feet when the big dog went into his protective maneuvers.

Drew uttered a one-word command in a foreign language. German, maybe?

The dog desisted, but stood at high alert, hackles raised, nose pointed forward, legs apart. He might be quiet, but his posture said he was ready to do whatever proved necessary to get the job done.

"Kimberly, you've never seen Rocky in action." Sympathy laced Amy's voice. "Are you okay?"

"Fine. Maybe. Somewhat."

"Sorry." Drew darted a quick look of apology her way as he steered the SUV down the exit driveway. "I should have explained that Rocky's trained to react to uninvited guests. My bad. We weren't scheduled to meet with anyone there, were we?"

"No. I expect that's a vineyard worker, coming to see what we are doing or if we need anything."

"The hill's angle and the height of the grapevines combined so we didn't see him until the last possible minute." Drew pulled out onto the road and headed south. "There's no way we can have enough people to keep that venue safe, not to mention the photography session at the historic grotto and then around the tip of the lake to the reception site at the inn. There just aren't numbers enough to make that feasible when you're talking political dignitaries, country music stars and a European royal family, half of whom come equipped with their own security teams that will, most likely, get in our way."

"Excuse me for asking," Kimberly began, and when Drew's frown said she probably shouldn't ask, she did anyway. "But wouldn't this wedding be easier to pull off after the elections?"

"It would have been easier a year ago when Rick was just testing the waters of candidacy," he replied as he turned south. "But now that he looks like the probable winner, there is no good time for eight years, assuming reelection. Which means we make do with the best we can do here, now. Why didn't they pick one of those gracious old churches in town? Don't people get married in sweet, historic churches anymore?"

Kimberly tapped her mother's notebook. "Shelby made the very good point that by doing it in town, the regular fall traffic, paparazzi and fans would clog the roads, and they'd never get to the photo ops or the reception site, which is true. A bottleneck around The Square is a logistical nightmare during festivals. They'd have to block off roads, and that would cut into sales revenue for local small businesses. It was really nice of her to see it that way." Their quaint, historic shopping area drew three-season tourist traffic, but major events challenged mobility, and that wasn't something to be shrugged off for a wedding like Shelby's.

"There aren't any festivals the weekend they picked, are there?"

"No, but leaf peepers will be out in full force."

"Good point." He sighed and started to turn toward the gracious nineteenth-century gardens Kate had booked for a post-ceremony photo session, but he paused when Kimberly put her hand on his arm. "Turn right instead."

"Because?"

"I just thought of something. If it works, we

might be able to give Shelby the wedding she wants and deserves and you some peace of mind."

Peace of mind?

With her hand on his arm, and the luminescent pearl polish glinting softly in the sun?

The scent of tropical fruit and flowers surprised him. At the office, he'd breathed in sugar and spice, but that must have been her mother's lingering preference.

Her proximity and the hand on his arm as he swung the wheel wafted the scent of tropical fruit salad with a hint of floral, just enough to say "feminine and proud of it" and fun enough to say she liked summer.

So did he.

"Turn left at the top of this hill."

He did what she asked, then nodded, remembering. "The Abbey."

"Gorgeous, right?"

"Magnificent building." Daryl peered out and whistled lightly. "Not much easy ingress or egress, plenty of parking, clear view on three sides. This is a wedding venue? How was it overlooked before?"

Kimberly climbed out and opened the back door for Amy. "Weddings, yes, on a limited basis, but no receptions. The friars sold the main building years ago, with certain stipulations to avoid commercialization. It's run by an area mission church, and they're fairly strict about usage in accordance with the friars' wishes, but renting the building for weddings and retreats and conferences allows them money to fund their work."

"So you're thinking we could do the ceremony here..."

"Let's check availability," Kimberly advised. "Uncle Steve is the church pastor. His daughter Tara oversees the calendar. Hopefully she's home."

"I remember Tara. She was like...twelve."

"Time marches on," Kimberly noted softly.

"Someone lives here?" Amy's eyes went wide as she eyed the broad, beautiful stone building with the impressive domed middle. "This would be like living in a castle."

"Which would be perfect because then I could put you in the dungeon," Drew agreed. "That way I'd know where you were, 24/7."

She laughed and clasped his hand as she exchanged a grin with Kimberly, and that brief moment made the sun seem brighter and the breeze sweeter.

"That view is amazing." Daryl waved east as he released Rocky from the back of the SUV. The terraced hillside gave way to the long, slim shoreline of Canandaigua Lake.

"Fabulous, right?" Kimberly smiled at Daryl's surprise, and when he looked over his shoulder at Drew and gave him a thumbs-up, she hoped the date was available. She climbed the steps and rang the bell outside the office door.

Almost instantly the window above them was pushed open. "Kimberly!"

"Tara, hey." She took a step back and looked up, but she was closer to the step's edge than she thought. When her three-inch heel missed concrete, she expected to crash to the pavement.

Two hands caught her waist, steadying her. And then for the sweetest of moments, they didn't let go. "You okay?"

That voice. Deep. Low. Caring. Always looking out for others. The combination of his grip, the tone and the whisper of his breath against her neck took her back to a time when life and love seemed simple. How much had changed since then.

"Yes. Thank you." She turned and looked straight into concerned, desert camo eyes, flecks of green, gold and brown vying for attention. Warrior eyes. "I'm glad you were there."

"Me, too."

Her heart did a physiologically impossible dance in her chest. She chalked it up to an adrenaline rush from the near fall and looked at him again.

"Don't fall!" Tara's face mixed joy and concern over Kimberly's lack of grace. "I'm coming right down. Kimberly, it's been forever!"

"Friendly little thing." Drew kept his tone low. "A bit out of step with the dignity of the surroundings, isn't she?"

"Whereas I would say she was happy to see her cousin after several years away and leave it at that."

Tara didn't come to the side door and open it for them. She stepped through the main doors leading into the friary, waited while they came across the tapered steps, then grabbed Kimberly in a hug. "Oh, I miss you! You look marvelous, and I was totally hoping you were planning to have the wedding in Grace Haven and would pick the Abbey. Kimberly, it will be beautiful!"

Drew paused inside the door. So did Daryl. They exchanged looks; then Drew turned, one brow hiked. "You're getting married?"

Right about then having the floor open up and swallow her whole would have gotten a preferential nod.

Didn't happen.

Kimberly shook her head and waved off Tara's words as she realized with her parents' current circumstances, word of her broken engagement hadn't been forwarded to the extended family. "Clearly I should have signed into social media last month and changed my status update." She held out a ringless left hand for Tara to see. "I won't be looking for a personal wedding venue anytime soon."

Tara winced. "Kimberly, I'm sorry. I had no idea."

Kimberly shrugged it off. "It's not a big deal. It's actually for the best, but thanks." She nodded toward Drew, Daryl and Amy. "Tara, this is Drew Slade, his daughter, Amy, and his security partner, Daryl Jackson. We're helping a client prepare for her wedding, and our first venue doesn't allow for the level of security we need. Then I thought of the Abbey."

"And I'm glad you did," Tara declared. "Drew, good to see you again," she continued in an easy tone. "It's been a long time," she added, then motioned toward the office wing. "Shall we check dates first or tour the building?"

"Tour." Drew's ease at taking charge said he did it often. Would that take-charge attitude extend to overthrowing all the bride's decisions? Kimberly aimed a frown his way.

He ignored it completely.

"Come this way." Tara moved down the spacious entry hall. Daryl and Amy fell in behind Tara, and somehow Drew ended up alongside Kimberly. He turned her way as they walked and kept his voice low. "Who broke it off?"

He did not just ask that, did he? As if it was his business? Because it wasn't. Remembering the price tag on this gig and the cost of her father's experimental treatment in Houston made her smile and play nice when she longed to tell Drew Slade to mind his own business. She couldn't do that, so she shrugged lightly. "He did."

Drew studied her for long, thick seconds, long enough for her heart to do that step-toe dance again. Then he leaned closer. "He's a moron, Kimber, but I might just send him a thank-you note."

Kimberly was pretty sure her breathing paused as their eyes met. "For?"

He winked.

Her heart stuttered, or was that her lungs? Maybe both, because Drew Slade had just flirted with her. Sure, he was just trying to ease an awkward moment, but that one brief exchange was enough to stir up those old schoolgirl feelings.

But that was then and this was now, and a whole lot of ugly had passed under their respective bridges.

Tara waited for them to catch up. "Exactly whose wedding are we planning?"

"Shelby Vandeveld's," Kimberly replied.

"That's a name that raises the stakes somewhat, doesn't it?" Tara moved toward the chapel area. "As you can see, we have adequate space and generous surroundings to host events up to three hundred people. But the core of our allure lies in the chapel, of course."

Daryl jotted notes as they walked.

Drew didn't. In contrast, he studied the venue from top to bottom as they toured the gracious old building. When Tara ended with the domed chapel, Drew paused just inside the door. "Stunning."

"One of the best kept secrets of the Finger Lakes," Tara agreed.

Drew shoulder-nudged Kimberly. "You're brilliant."

"Save the praise until we mesh dates. I'm sure they have several fall retreats scheduled."

"We do, so let's move to my office and see what we've got," Tara suggested.

They moved to the office, where Tara drew up an electronic calendar on her desktop. When Drew gave her the date, she shook her head quickly. "Not available for that weekend or the one before. We have a Sunday open the second week of October…"

"Just Sunday?"

She met Drew's eye and nodded.

"We need a seventy-two-hour clean date."

If asking for a three-day security window on popular venues mere weeks ahead of time surprised Tara, she covered it well. "Nothing in October."

Kimberly had expected that answer, so when Tara paged back to September, she was surprised.

"We had a retreat cancellation," Tara explained, and she tapped the calendar in front of her. "We actually have a four-day window in September as a result. Would your reception venue be available then?"

Drew frowned. "Most likely not." He scrubbed a hand over the back of his neck. "I should have anticipated Rick's candidacy and been here at the first meeting between your mother and Shelby. The blame for this is coming straight to my door."

Kimberly looked at Tara. "How many people were supposed to be at the canceled retreat?"

"Just shy of three hundred." She studied Kimberly's face and cringed as if reading her mind. "You know the rules, Kim."

"How many Indonesian missions is Holy Name Church supporting right now?"

"Three."

"A price tag like this could double that option and fulfill a patriotic duty. If we don't figure this out, I've got a very nice bride who's being robbed of her wedding day because she had the nerve to fall in love at a politically incorrect time. Where's Uncle Steve?"

"He's at the church food cupboard in Prattsburgh."

"Would he mind a visit?"

"From you? Never. But don't be disappointed if he has to say no."

"What are we asking him, exactly?" Drew faced the two women directly. "The lack of dates puts this out of the question, doesn't it? Maybe we should consider just having the wedding, pictures and reception at the inn and be done with it."

"That's a last-resort answer to an ongoing unresolved problem," Kimberly chided him. "Let me go talk to Uncle Steve, and we'll see if we can make this right."

"There's nothing wrong with the inn plan, Kimber."

Drew leveled that stubborn cop gaze her way. Her heart wanted to step closer, smooth the irritation that creased his brow again, but her head kept her right where she belonged, four distinct feet away. "If what Shelby wanted was an everyday wedding, that's what she would have planned and that would be fine. But a woman who chose rose gardens and a grotto with an amazing view of Canandaigua Lake probably was looking for a perfect fall setting to match the colors she's picked for everything from flowers to linens to chair drapes. This won't be exactly what she dreamed about, but it would be something special. Let me talk to Uncle Steve and see what he says."

"About?"

"Maybe doing the whole thing right here."

That piqued his interest. Daryl's, too. He looked intrigued and nodded. "That would solvc a myriad of problems, pretty lady."

"But you said it was against the rules." Drew included Tara in his statement, but Kimberly answered.

"It is, technically, but there's nothing holier than the blessing of matrimony. Uncle Steve's got the final say, but this could work. Of course, we'd have to let the other venue know—"

"No."

She turned toward Drew, surprised. "No? What do you mean?"

"If this works out, if your uncle agrees, then we keep the other venue listed."

Daryl nodded again. "The perfect red herring."

"Yes. We'd pay them, of course, but losing the cost of that is worth the added security we'd get by bringing everyone into town four weeks earlier than we originally planned. He turned toward Tara. "How's your security on that computer?"

She raised a spiral-bound notebook and asked, "What computer?"

He grinned, and when he did his face shed years of worry. "You've done this before."

"We've hosted some big names in the last five years. Knowing when to go old-school and leave no electronic footprint has been helpful."

"You're talking our language."

"But first." Kimberly reached out her hand for the keys. "I need the keys to go see Uncle Steve."

He could have just tossed her the keys. He didn't. He turned toward Tara. "With your permission, I'd like Daryl and Rocky to stay here and familiarize themselves with the layout. And if you two don't mind, can I leave Amy here so I'm not distracted while I meet your dad?"

She laughed and hooked a thumb toward the east wing. "My mother made cookies last night when things cooled off. Amy and I can grab some and talk girl stuff so Daryl can get his work done."

Amy hesitated, mock-concerned. "There is no dungeon, right? Because Dad might have an ulterior motive for leaving me here."

Drew grinned, and once again Kimberly glimpsed the guy he'd been before drug dealers had gunned his partner down in the street. "Then be extra good, honey. Just in case." He turned back to Kimberly. "Let's go."

"You really feel the need to watch me coax my uncle into opening the Abbey for the reception?"

He strode past her, through the door and toward the car. "No surprises, remember? Like it or not, Kimber." He turned and faced her over the roof of the SUV. "We're attached at the hip for a while."

"What about the senator? Who's protecting him and the family if you and Daryl are here?"

"He's under Secret Service jurisdiction now. When it comes to this wedding?" He pointed to her, then hooked a thumb back toward himself. "It's you and me."

His serious expression held her gaze, but then he did the unthinkable.

He smiled.

And in that smile she saw a glimmer of hope she hadn't noticed in the first two hours they were together. It brightened his eyes and relaxed his jaw, letting her glimpse the old Drew she'd liked so well back in the day.

Her phone rang. She checked the display and saw her sister-in-law's name. Dave's widow, Corinne, left to raise her toddler son and unborn daughter on her own. A single parent driven by circumstances she might not have faced if Drew had gotten to the appointed meeting place on time.

She answered the call, still facing Drew. "Corinne, hey! What's up? How are the kids?"

The sound of Corinne's name accomplished her goal.

Guilt replaced Drew's smile. She'd done it purposely to remind him of what her family had lost at his hands.

He climbed into the car, waited while she finished the call, then started the engine once she was seated. Hands tight on the steering wheel, he aimed the car south and drove to the little town of Prattsburgh without saying a word.

She'd changed his easy mood intentionally, and now she had a twenty-minute drive to ponder what she'd done. When they finally pulled into the parking lot of the small stone church, she figured that might have been the longest twenty minutes of her life, and it was all her fault.

A roadside sign invited people to the weekend services. Beneath the listed times was one simple quote: "Blessed are the peacemakers, for they shall be called children of God."

The tight line of Drew's jaw indicated she needed a whole lot of work in the peacemaker department. He waited while she moved ahead, not meeting her gaze.

Shame coursed through her. Her parents and sisters had never blamed Drew. Now, seeing his reaction to Corinne's call, Kimberly glimpsed a hollowness inside him, an emptiness that reflected her own. Her shallow move had opened a fresh chasm between them, and she had no clue how to fix it.

She turned as Uncle Steve came through the church door. When he welcomed Drew with a big hug, she felt worse than ever.

Blessed are the peacemakers...

The sign taunted her. Seeing Uncle Steve's hearty welcome to an old family friend spoke volumes. The rest of the family had moved on, long ago. Why couldn't she?

Because you were mad at Dave when he died. He'd scolded you about being self-absorbed, and you hung up on him.

And then he was gone. Just gone. And no amount of apology could bring him back or fix that last fateful call.

"Kimberly!" Uncle Steve's robust voice jerked her back into the here and now. As she stepped past Drew to hug her father's brother, guilt still bit deep. She'd been a jerk, then and now. Could she change?

Sure, if she wanted to badly enough. One way or another, she needed to come to peace with three things while she was back in Grace Haven. The loss of her beloved brother and a sweeter relationship with her two sisters headed the list. And the other?

She sighed inside.

The other was finding a common ground with Drew Slade. From the set of his jaw right now, that one didn't look the least bit likely.

Chapter Three

"I can't believe you talked him into it." Drew made sure Kimberly heard the approval in his tone. "I'm impressed."

She shrugged as she fastened her seat belt and checked her lipstick. She pulled out some shade that looked like ripe, sweet cherries and applied a fresh coat.

Drew's pulse ramped, but this was Dave's sister. Old angst and harsh feelings lay solidly between them. Ogling her beautiful mouth and her pretty smile didn't make the short list.

"You knew he'd cave."

"I knew he'd see the common sense of the situation," she corrected him as she put the lipstick away. "Uncle Steve's ministries are very important to their congregation, and money is crucial to aid. He knows my parents are in a rough spot with a lot of unexpected out-of-pocket expenses, so making one exception to help Mom's business, the next president's daughter and the bottom line of the mission collections was a no-brainer. While he's a great preacher—"

"Always was," Drew noted.

Her smile said she agreed. "He comprehends that little gets done in Indonesia without funds, and the price tag on Shelby's wedding will keep those three churches and a clinic running for a year."

Drew whistled, then he stopped the car. "Look." He waited while she lifted her gaze, and the smile he'd hoped to inspire said she remembered this location from two decades before.

"We spent a lot of time racing up and down those hills," he reminded her.

"That old toboggan was a death trap," she remembered. "But not nearly as crazy as those circular sleds that went like lightning. How did we survive?"

"The way most kids do, I suppose." He studied the long sloping hill and pointed left. "Do you think Harv still makes the best hot chocolate?"

"I don't know. I haven't gone sledding since..." Her voice tapered off. Her smile diminished.

Drew read the timeline. She hadn't gone sledding since Dave died. Neither had he. He'd gone off, striving to fill his life with all kinds of things, but in the end he realized he'd totally become a mess-up and that was that.

And then Rick Vandeveld hired him to do security for his online trading facility downstate. Rick had believed in Drew long before Drew believed in himself again. "Amy would love this."

"What kid wouldn't?" She turned and asked the question he knew was coming. "When did you get married, Drew? Because I never heard a word about it."

It was time to come clean on an old indiscretion. "I didn't."

"Oh." She stared at the old sledding hill. "Well, Amy's beautiful and smart and so much like you that it's like having a feminine version. She looks like a princess, but she's got a warrior mentality."

"She does." He gazed at the sledding hill, too. He started to speak, then paused. Kimberly didn't need to hear his tale of woe. She had her own worries. Life had dealt her a rough couple of months. He was pretty sure she could use a break. He knew he could. "And I have no idea what I'm going to do with her while we're here. She was supposed to be at camp and then back at school."

"She didn't sound all too thrilled about the idea of boarding school."

"That was just for this term, while Rick gets

situated in Washington, but obviously that plan's been tossed. I'm due back at V-Trade the first of the year, running security."

"And V-Trade is?"

He couldn't believe she hadn't heard of them, which meant he'd talk to Rick about targeting investment-minded women with better-placed advertising. "Online trading corporation. We specialize in cutting out the middle man by using low-priced trading software. We've got offices in Manhattan and just outside of Newark."

"Crazy population density." She lifted her eyes from the sprawling hill to his. "Doesn't that feel weird after growing up here?"

He couldn't deny it, but the frenetic pace of Manhattan had helped heal old wounds. He hadn't had time to think about them, much less let them fester. "It was a gradual upward climb. That helped. And maybe being so different was good therapy. Rick started small, the business mushroomed and I was along for the ride. Then he became the state senator. And now?" He tightened his jaw. "Rick's been on a fast track for years, but there's a part of me that's ready to slow things down."

"For Amy's sake."

He eased the car back onto the road. "For both of us. It's time for Team Slade to plant some roots. I don't want her entire childhood messed up by my constant comings and goings."

"Who watches her when you're home?"

"My neighbor. She's a nice woman—bakes cookies. And she loves Amy. But she and her husband are relocating to Florida this year."

"Making it the perfect time to make a change."

He'd thought the exact same thing. "Yes. Moving is hard on kids, but Amy's resilient. And as you noticed earlier, she's not exactly feeling the whole 'in crowd' thing when she's farmed out to upscale venues."

"I got that. So let me make you an offer."

"I'm listening."

"Let Amy hang out with Emily or Rory or Allison at the office when you and I are working on something where she can't tag along."

"That's—"

She must have sensed his quick refusal because one hand—one soft, sweet hand—touched his mouth and he quieted down right quick as she spoke for him. "That's a great idea, Kimberly. Amy will love learning about bridal parties and planning, and I won't have to worry about her."

She moved her hand, but the summer scent lingered, making him think of sandy beaches, bonfires and coconut-scented sunscreen. And Kimberly. "You really think that would be okay?"

"I know it would be okay or I wouldn't have offered," she replied sensibly. "Rory's doing volunteer work for migrants when she's not helping us. She's running a summer pre-K program over in the elementary school."

"A missionary at heart, like your uncle Steve."

"Yes. I'm sure Amy would enjoy helping with the little kids each morning. It's only got a couple more weeks, but that would keep Amy busy half the day, and the other half could be at the office. Problem solved."

"You've gotten bossier as you've matured." He liked that about her. Kimberly had always been the go-to Gallagher, the one who planned her work, then worked her plan. "No wonder you're so good at what you do."

Drew's words hit two distinct notes. She was good at her job, and she had gotten bossy. She didn't always like that side of herself, but quick decision making had been a mainstay for years. "A necessity when making quick assessments."

"Amen to that."

"Where are you and Daryl staying?"

"The Country Inn."

"Might I suggest moving to the B and B on Iroquois Avenue?" She turned to face him. His profile, older, more mature, more focused than she remembered, but dear in its familiarity even when she didn't want it to be. "You'd be right in town with a great view of The Square and the water. Everything is within walking distance. And that way Amy can duck back to her room now and again if she needs a break."

"Alone?" He pulled the car into the Abbey's empty parking lot and turned. "Not gonna happen."

"How old is Amy?"

"Eleven."

"What were you doing in Grace Haven at age eleven, Drew?" She knew the answer, and his grimace said he got her drift. At age eleven he and Dave had had village paper routes, they'd drummed up quick baseball and soccer games at the town park and had ridden their bikes wherever two boys wanted to go. "I rest my case."

"Amy wasn't raised here. Her environment's been more protected."

"By necessity." Kimberly slung her purse over her shoulder once she stepped out. "Life's different in Grace Haven. Let her get a taste of that while she's here."

"Hey!" Excited, Amy dashed down the steps to meet them. Her shoulder-length, dirty-blond hair lightened in the midday sun, and her smile brightened the moment. "Your uncle said yes! He called Tara and we're good to go!"

"Who needs a town crier when I've got you?"

Drew put his finger to his lips. “Bear in mind the sensitivity of this event, okay? You can’t chat about it, or tell your friends back home what’s going on. Even if you’re tempted. Get it?”

“Cross my heart.”

“Tara, I know we kind of sprung this on you,” Kimberly said as Tara and Daryl reached them at a more deliberate pace. “Can you and I sit down—”

“With me and Daryl,” Drew intoned. “Remember?”

“You won’t possibly let me forget,” Kim shot back. When he smiled, she wasn’t sure if she should smack him or hug him, which meant even though she had to work side by side with Drew for the coming weeks, she’d be keeping her distance. She’d had her fill of cops and cop types, and every time she looked at Drew she pictured Dave by his side. Laughing. Scolding. Teasing.

But Dave wasn’t there anymore. She’d never apologized to her brother for dismissing his concerns before he died, and then he was gone and it was too late. Between her reality TV–style summer in Nashville and her father’s health battles, Kimberly couldn’t handle anything else. She tapped her electronic notebook. “Would you prefer I keep hard copy notes, as well?”

“Yes, ma’am.”

The way he said it, as if deferring to her when

the opposite was true, almost made her smile. And when he grasped his daughter's hand and moved back toward the wide stone steps, the sight of father and daughter brought back good memories. Not enough to fully cloak the bad ones, but enough to bring a hint of peace to her heart.

She'd relish that sweet peace for however long it lasted, which with a stubborn man like Drew might be five minutes. But it was five minutes she intended to enjoy.

"Next step—food." Tara had hooked Kimberly up with a spiral-bound notebook. Drew aimed the car back onto Route 14 while she scribbled notes forty-five minutes later.

"Do you really think that the florist, linen supply company, caterers and all the rest can keep quiet about this?"

"They can. *Will* they?" Kimberly shrugged. "We'll see. But if everything is being done under assumed names, the date is changed and the other venue on hold, we've got a good start. So back to food."

"You're hungry?" Drew turned her way once he was headed north. "Because I'm starved, and I'm sure the kid could eat something. And Daryl's hungry by nature."

"And not too proud to admit it," Daryl assured them from the backseat.

"Then let's kill two birds with one stone." Kimberly didn't look up as she sketched something in the pages of the book. "Josie Gallagher's got the best barbecue this side of the Mason-Dixon Line, and if you think we don't know 'cue in New York, you'd be wrong. Let's go get lunch, and we'll check out her catering menu."

"For?"

"The wedding, of course."

Drew winced. "I'm not sure that Shelby and her mother are the barbecue type."

"So now we're worried about the bride all of a sudden." He didn't have to look sideways to know the look she aimed his way was less than friendly. "Bear in mind that half the guest list is from the South, and they love barbecue. And in country music, good old-fashioned food ranks mighty high. In any case, this is a moot point until we've had you guys taste Josie's food. She's on Fourth Street, right along the lakefront, just beyond the state boat-launching facility."

Drew knew that area. There used to be a funny old diner there, rustic and run-down as the owner aged.

When he turned into the restaurant parking lot ten minutes later, the difference amazed him. "Great place."

"Right?" She turned and smiled at him. When she did, years rolled back, a bunch of friends, hanging out, grabbing a burger, having a swim. "Josie hired Jon Robilard to do the repairs and upgrades. He brought the whole retro/rustic look back to life."

"What is that smell?" Daryl breathed deep as he came around the car, and the look of appreciation on his face made Kimberly laugh.

"That's Josie's way of welcoming you and your taste buds to Bayou Barbecue. Let's go see what's cooking."

"It doesn't matter." Drew pulled the door open and held it as the rest stepped through. "Anything that smells this good has to be amazing."

It was. They sampled outlaw potatoes, baked to perfection and stuffed with sour cream, cheese and home-cured bacon. Brisket, sliced thin, perfectly smoked, fork tender. Ribs, full flavored and messy, served with a side of a warm, wet washcloth for a quick tableside cleanup. Cheesy corn casserole, an old-time favorite. Cajun chicken. Cajun fish. Pecan pie and home-churned vanilla frozen custard, a town treasure and secret. "Josie bought a franchise from Stan to produce his custard here."

"No way would Stan Richardson franchise out his business." Drew's dad and Stan's son had been good friends before his parents had passed away. "I can't believe it."

"Josie's pretty convincing," Kimberly told him, then waved her cousin over as the lunch crowd thinned. "Josie, come here and meet these guys, and if you have a minute, sit and talk with us about event catering."

"Coffee first," Josie declared. She made herself a cup and brought a fresh pot to the table along with a tray with four mugs. "I no longer assume that tweens and teens don't drink coffee because a lot of them do."

Amy laughed as she reached for a mug. "I love coffee and lattes."

"Children of a new millennium," Drew muttered. He didn't dissuade the choice of beverage, which might mean he was a terrible parent, but he'd been drinking coffee himself since age twelve. And he was doing okay. Most days.

Josie sank into a chair, leaned back and sighed. "Crazy, busy lunch hour."

"You can say that again." Daryl smiled at her as he motioned to the kitchen area behind the fast-paced call-in counter. "Best barbecue I've had in years. And I've had a lot of 'cue in my time."

Josie beamed. "I love hearing that. Thank you…?" She raised a brow, waiting for Daryl's name, and Drew's partner wasted no time. His quick appreciative smile said he was mighty pleased to meet her. Of course, the woman was quite good-looking, and that might have helped spike Daryl's grin of appreciation.

"Daryl Jackson." Josie shook Daryl's hand as he indicated Drew with a quick thumb in Drew's direction. "We're on consultation in the area for a couple of months, and I can already predict where I'll be eating for the duration."

"Music to every restaurant owner's ears." Josie exchanged smiles with him, then turned to Amy. "I'm Josie Gallagher, Kimberly's cousin. And you are?"

"Amy Slade. This is my dad, Drew. And I have to agree with Uncle Daryl. That was the best barbecue I've ever had. In my entire life."

Drew cleared his throat, and Josie laughed. "My guess is you haven't had as much as you think, but why not start with the best?"

"Which brings me right back to the matter at hand," Kimberly told her. "I'm bidding on a last-minute late-September function and I think a multicourse, down-home Southern barbecue would be amazing."

"As long as the hosts approve it," Drew interrupted. "We don't want to make assumptions on their behalf."

They didn't? Because wasn't that exactly what Shelby had empowered her to do? Make things work? And now Drew was flexing muscle in the other direction as if they needed to run things by the bride and her mother. Which Kimberly had every intention of doing, so why was he interfering?

Oh. Wait. Because he was Drew Slade—that's why. Bossy, assertive and a pain in the neck at the moment, no matter how good he looked in that ribbed black T-shirt and khakis. She sent him a long, cool look, an expression that she hoped telegraphed the feelings behind her words. "Of course, we need approvals, but there's no way of getting them without pricing, is there, Josie?"

"No, ma'am." Josie looked from Kimberly to Drew and back again, then smiled. "Give me the specs, and I'll draw up an estimate with a suggested menu for you by Monday. I'd promise it earlier, but we're in the thick of boating and tourist season, and anyone who operates a business in the North knows you make money when you can, as you can."

"How soon would you need confirmation to be able to handle a crowd just shy of three hundred people in five weeks?"

"I'd want firm numbers in ten days. I need time to order the proper cuts and smoke things appropriately. Do we need to do a tasting?"

"Just did." Kimberly's smile said she thought

Josie's food passed with flying colors. "Awesome, as usual."

"Crazy Leon doesn't let just anyone into his kitchen on the bayou, nor does he release you into the food prep world without making sure you can actually do the job."

"You worked for Leon?" Daryl hiked both brows, surprised at the mention of one of the barbecue greats. "My mama went to school with him back in the day. She said he was born with a spatula in his hand and a nose for combination elements."

Josie laughed. "That's him, all right. I worked for Leon for eight years before I realized I couldn't handle one more Cajun summer. Not when Canandaigua Lake was calling my name. I relocated here about four years back, and we're doing okay."

"That makes three of you that came home," Amy noted.

Kimberly turned. So did Drew, Daryl and Josie.

"Kimberly, Dad and you," she continued, looking up at Josie. "It must be a pretty nice place to be if you all end up coming back, right?"

"Except we're only here on temporary consulting assignment, and Kimberly's here because her dad is sick," Drew explained. "Only Josie came back on a permanent basis."

"There must be something that calls people back, Dad," Amy argued. "You read it in books all the time. You see it in movies. As if people kind of need to get away, but they leave part of themselves there. In their hometown. And then they come back."

The kid had made a great point, so why were her words so tough to hear? Maybe because they were true. Kimberly slung an arm around Amy's shoulders in a half hug.

"I like your sentimental side," she told her. "The opposite of your dad. And you know something I've discovered?"

"What?" Amy looked up, interested. So did Josie and Daryl. Drew drew his brows together, frowning. Because she thought him dispassionate? Or because Amy was sentimental?

"I forgot how nice this town is. The funny stores and mix of tourists. The traffic around The Square, the endless parade of people at the beach and the five old guys who hang out on the corner of Market and Vine, smoking cigars and playing cards while they watch the world pass by."

"You're making a group of feisty old men into a selling point?" Skepticism marked Drew's words. "That's a stretch."

"It's Grace Haven." Kim shrugged. "I think

when you're away you get used to a new normal and you forget to appreciate how cool the old normal was. That's all I'm saying."

"Well, Pretty Polly sure thinks enough of those fellows to make sure she strolls down Center Street every morning at nine-fifty. Unless it's raining or a blizzard," Josie offered, grinning.

"You get blizzards here?" Amy's voice hiked up. "We get a little snow once in a while in Jersey, but I've always dreamed of snowy winters. Sledding. Skating."

"Shoveling." Drew looked unamused. He stood and turned toward the door as if he couldn't wait to escape. "Josie, nice meeting you. I'll look forward to hearing from you."

"We'll look forward to it," Kimberly corrected him. "You've got my number, Josie."

"I'll be in touch," Josie promised. Kimberly would have to be blind not to see her cousin's look of amusement. Amused at her? Drew? The whole situation?

At the moment, she wasn't finding Drew humorous, approachable or all that friendly, and that was gonna make for a long five weeks.

Chapter Four

Amy likes Grace Haven.

Drew got that. Amy had a case of small-town-itis, wishing for roots, although the snow lament was only because she hadn't stood in the school-bus loop for ten minutes in a snow squall, freezing to death, or shoveled dozens of driveways to make a few extra bucks. Her snow info had been pretty much relegated to nonstop Christmas movies on the inspirational channel, hope and dreams decked out in red, green and staged snow. So she was loving the *thought* of her father's hometown, while Drew was taking a deep breath with every old face he saw. In their eyes he read the timeline. They remembered him ramming around town, him and Dave, best buds, always together.

And Dave was gone.

He dropped Kim at the office and drove the

SUV around to the Country Inn. As he exited the car, Kimberly's words came back to him. He hesitated, glanced at Amy, then pulled out his phone to get the number for the bed-and-breakfast. On this point, Kimberly was right. If Amy was going to be in town for more than a month, it made no sense to have a hotel room on the highway when they could be right in the walking district. He called the B and B to check on vacancies and when the owner heard the time frame, Drew thought she squeaked in excitement. "Six weeks?"

"At least that. And we'll pay in advance."

"We've got room," the woman declared. "I can have it ready for you about seven tonight. Is that all right?"

"Perfect." He turned to Daryl as he hung up the phone. "You okay with staying here at the inn?"

"I am." Daryl smiled down at Amy. "I think Amy will love living in town, in walking distance to everything—"

"As long as she follows my rules," boomed Drew in a voice meant to scare her silly.

It did no such thing. She grinned up at him, looped her arm through his and hugged it. "I've never been able to walk anywhere on my own. Ever. Not in New Jersey, not in Manhattan. This is like a dream come true, Dad. A normal life, even if it's just for a little while."

It wasn't a dream come true for Drew, but that wasn't important now. Amy was important. And Shelby's wedding, keeping it flawless. If he had to face old demons, then it was time to face them. He thought he'd come to terms with Dave's death, he'd have argued the point if asked, but coming back to Grace Haven and seeing old sights, sounds and people cut deep.

Maybe they're supposed to.

He ignored the internal twinge and tossed Daryl a burner phone. "Let's switch things up again."

Daryl pocketed the phone and headed inside. Drew checked his watch, saw they had over two hours until the B and B could accommodate them and pointed Amy to the car. "Hop in. I'm going to give you the grand tour."

"Really?" Excitement lit her voice, as if trolling around a one-horse Finger Lakes town was some big deal.

"Yes."

"I'll love it, Dad!"

Her eagerness made him smile. Top to bottom, stem to stern, she'd be in her glory because Grace Haven, New York, was small-town perfection. Safe, beautiful, historic, inviting… You name it, Grace Haven had it. Depth of beauty, something not every old town could claim.

His words brought Kimberly's face to mind. *The beautiful Gallagher girl...* That's how he'd always thought of her, once she'd gotten past the pesky adolescent awkward stage.

She was still pesky. But she'd only gotten more beautiful, and how was he supposed to not notice that?

He didn't have a clue.

He took Amy on a rolling tour of the town, then paused by the water park. "If you cause no trouble tomorrow, we'll get an evening pass and spend tomorrow evening here," he promised. "But that means no trouble at all, kid."

She ticked off her fingers. "No hitchhiking, no drugs, alcohol, boys."

Drew firmed his jaw, his voice and his grim expression to the very maximum of his abilities. "No boys. Ever. Got it?"

She laughed and hugged him. "They're icky. Yuck."

She'd said the same thing for years, but one of these days—sooner, rather than later, no doubt—her eyes would be opened and she'd think boys were kind of cool.

Dungeon time.

He just needed to be in a location with accessibility to old stone basements. Luckily almost every house in the village sported one of those, so he was in good hands for a while.

"Can we walk?"

"We sure can." He parked the car in the shade, left it running to keep it cool for the dog, then took her hand as they strolled through the quaint, historic business district. "This is The Square."

"This rocks!" Amy stood in the middle of the town square and spun. "Cars actually go in a square pattern! Who thought of such an awesome thing? It's like an old movie, Dad."

"I think a lot of old towns had squares or circles in the middle."

"Really? As awesome as this one?" She pointed in each direction. "Kimberly's shop is there. Then there's clothing, ice cream, bakery, bookstore, hardware store, jewelry, leather stuff." She ticked off the rest of the shops on her fingers, amazed. "And a park in the middle of it all."

"It wasn't quite this fancy when I was your age." He sat on one of the metal-and-wood park benches and looked around.

"No?" Amy took a seat next to him. "But the buildings are old, so they were here."

"They were, but a lot of the stores are different now. Artsy and trendy, filled with things to buy."

"Isn't that the point?"

He laughed because it was. "When I was a

kid there were two accountants, a dry cleaners, a little drugstore, a print shop and two dentists added into the mix, so it wasn't the surround-all shopping experience you see. This is like a fancy old-fashioned strip mall now, catering to the tourist's pocketbook."

"That would be a lot different," Amy agreed. "I like this better."

"So does the tourism council, I expect. When I was in college they actually officially named this area 'The Square,' and people come from all over to shop here. Except for midwinter, these shops probably do a killer business. Are you hungry yet?"

She shook her head. "Too much lunch. Although I wouldn't say no to an ice-cream supper."

"Ice cream it is." He clasped her hand as they crossed the shaded park, a perfect respite for midday breaks and late-day repose. They got into line at Stan's Frozen Custard, and he was just thinking how nice it was to not have to talk when someone poked him in the back. Drew had to remind himself that you didn't necessarily have to draw your weapon when turning around in Grace Haven. He turned, and it took a few seconds to recognize the youngest Gallagher girl. "Rory?"

"Drew." She grabbed him in a big hug, just

like Emily had done. "It's so good to have you home again. And this must be Amy." Rory high-fived Amy with a quick smile. "I'm Kimberly's youngest sister. She said she had a ball with you today."

"I had fun, too. Kimberly's great."

Rory waved that off. "Well, we won't share that or it'll go to her head, and the last thing my big sister needs is anyone else telling her how awesome she is. There'll be no living with her then, and it's no piece of cake now."

Amy laughed, but Drew wondered how much of Rory's spiel was humor and how much truth. Dave used to cringe when his sisters would go at it over almost anything. Drew was an only child, he'd never had to worry about getting along or sharing or doing chores together. Kind of like Amy now. He knew that wasn't a bad thing… but he wasn't sure it was a good thing, either.

Rory studied Amy, tapping a finger to her jaw. "You're in town for a while, right?"

Amy sent a guilty-as-charged look up to her father, then nodded. "Yes."

"I was wondering…" Rory played the moment as if she'd just come up with a great plan and hadn't talked this all out with her older sister. Drew knew better. "I teach at a UPK in the mornings until Labor Day."

"A UP what?"

"Universal prekindergarten, to help kids get ready for school."

"Oh, with little kids. I love little kids!" Amy shot a look up at Drew, one of those "I'd love to have brothers and sisters" expressions he'd learned to ignore years before.

"Really?" Rory's brows shot up, and Drew had to hand it to her. She was playing the part to the max and doing it well. "How would you feel about helping me there in the mornings, and then helping Emily, Allison and Kimberly out in the offices in the afternoons?"

"Are you serious?"

"On occasion." Rory smiled at her. "I missed the whole event planner/wedding planner gene thing, I'm not even all that big on weddings. That's a lot of money and time invested on one crazy day."

"The family maverick," Drew noted as they moved closer to the ice-cream ordering window. "Rory, what would you like? It's on me."

Rory didn't hesitate, and that was another difference between her and Kimberly. Kimberly would have weighed the idea of him buying ice cream, the motives behind it on both sides.

Rory just liked ice cream.

"A hot fudge sundae with mint chocolate chip custard. Please."

"Dad, can I have the same only with the red raspberry ice cream?"

"Is that a thing?"

Amy grinned. "It is now. Hey, look. There's Kimberly. Kimberly, hi! We're over here!"

Kimberly turned from locking the office door and spotted them. Her instant smile made Drew feel better about almost everything. She walked their way, slanted a look down to Amy, then up to Drew. "She doesn't make undercover easy, does she?"

Amy winced, chagrined, while Drew nodded. "She sure doesn't. Which made Camp Wellington attractive."

"Sorry." Amy put up her hands, palms out. "I totally promise to tone things down. I can do it. I just forget when I get excited."

"Excitement and youth should always go hand-in-hand," Kimberly told her. "Having an ice-cream supper, I take it?"

"Yes. Have one with us," Amy implored. "Rory's going to. And Dad's buying."

He was so certain she'd refuse that he was ready to smooth it over. When Kimberly turned, looked him straight in the eye and arched one amazingly perfect brow, he was pretty sure his heart went into abnormal sinus rhythm…and it felt great. "You know how to clinch a deal, Amy Sue Slade. I'm in. I would love a—"

"Banana split with chopped walnuts and three cherries."

She held his gaze. Or he held hers. He really wasn't sure which way it happened, but then she touched one hand to her throat as if unsure what to do and smiled. "You remembered."

He did. He used to tease her about the huge triple-scoop sundae when all the other girls ordered "baby" sized cones.

Not Kimberly. Not ever.

She touched her throat again, almost…nervous? Because he remembered?

That thought made him smile inside, because he remembered a lot of things about Kimberly Gallagher, things he'd pushed aside because she'd been so angry after Dave's death.

To everything there is a season...

One of his favorite Bible verses, simple and true. A time for healing, maybe? Maybe long past time. And most definitely a time to set old wrongs to rights and have ice cream on a sun-soaked August night.

"Can a person be too full to walk?" Amy wondered as they retrieved Rocky from the cool car a little while later. "Because that might be the case on my part."

Kimberly laughed. "That makes the walk imperative. Is Dad going to show you around town?"

"The rest of it, yes." Drew tossed his paper cup into the garbage can nearby. "We've got a little while before we can check in at the B and B."

"You called them." Silly how a little thing like that made her happy, a simple thing like following her suggestion.

"Having Amy in town makes sense," he admitted. "So after I thought about it, weighed the options and gave it enough time to become my own idea, I called." His wry expression said the admission was painful.

Kimberly laughed. "Such a guy."

"Some people like that about me, Kimber."

Heat started somewhere around her middle and crept up because she wasn't exactly immune to Drew's magnetism. Something about six solid feet of broad-shouldered, focused, rugged man put a girl's defenses on high alert. Luckily she wasn't afraid to heed the warnings.

"Guys, I'm heading home." Seeming oblivious, Rory interrupted the moment. "I've got some prep work to do for tomorrow morning's session, and I want time for a late swim before I call it a day. Amy, I'll meet you here in the morning, okay? Is eight-fifty good for you, Drew?"

"Absolutely," he declared. "I'm grateful, Rory."

She waved that off as she headed north on Center Street. "No biggie. We'll have fun, and I get free help. Perfect!"

Drew turned back toward Amy. "So. Shall we turn right and explore the town buildings or left and walk along the lakeshore?"

She hesitated, then nodded to the right. "I want to see where everything is. That way I won't get lost if I go exploring."

"Good move." Kimberly started to move in the opposite direction, but Amy's voice made her think twice.

"Kimberly? You wanna walk with us?"

A part of her did. How peaceful and nice to walk the avenues of her past with Drew and his precocious daughter and the stately dog.

A bigger part wanted to run the other way. She'd had sensory overload just driving around the lake with Drew earlier. Strolling along the streets and places they used to hang out would be too much. Besides, she'd promised Corinne she'd watch Callan's baseball game at the town field. "I can't, but thank you, honey. I'll see you in the morning, okay?"

"I can't wait." Sincerity deepened the girl's smile, a smile just like her daddy's when he was a kid. Bright. Happy. Always on the move.

She walked down the narrow block to her car, started the engine, then paused. The town opened up before her, the lake to her left, the business and historic district to her right, with tree-lined neighborhoods stretching in every direction. She watched as Drew and Amy disappeared from view on Center Street, then sighed.

She was a fish out of water in her own hometown, and that was her own fault for staying away too long. Worse? She suspected Drew felt exactly the same way. They'd led two distinct lives in Grace Haven: A life set before Dave died, and another marked by laying him to rest.

Maybe moving away was a major mistake, because the people who stayed in town, the others who loved Dave…her parents, her sisters, Corinne, his friends…had moved on, while she and Drew were mired in thick guilt.

Her phone alarm reminded her of Callan's game. She put the car in gear. She passed a local church; the young pastor was outside the rectory, having a catch with a boy about five years old.

She wanted that. She hadn't realized how much until Phil broke their engagement. In retrospect, she knew he'd done the right thing. She didn't love Phil. Hadn't loved him. They'd worked well together on events, they liked a lot of the same things and he was a good guy, but they'd coasted into a status they thought everyone expected because all their Nashville buddies were tying the knot.

They'd been silly. Calling the wedding off made some kind of painful sense, but she didn't love biting back embarrassment every time she came face-to-face with folks who didn't know.

She pulled into the athletic field parking lot, found Corinne and her precocious niece and sank onto the bleachers next to them.

"Do you or do you not love this outfit, Aunt Kim?" Ten-year-old Tee asked, smiling widely.

Kimberly faced the delightful girl and grinned in appreciation. Her niece had been christened Theresa at birth, but Callan had shortened it to "Tee Tee" long ago, and the name fit. Tee Gallagher was looking for an over-the-top reaction. Kim did her justice. "Tee! Beyond adorable, bordering breathtaking, where on earth did you get it?"

"Goodwill." While so many little girls shopped designer stores at the big mall in Victor, Tee loved to celebrate a great bargain. "Five dollars and fifteen cents. Including socks I don't have on because I'm wearing flip-flops."

"I'm getting you a gig on QVC," Kimberly declared, laughing. "Corinne, she's got a great eye."

"And a rockin' affordable budget," Corinne agreed. She exchanged smiles with Kimberly and pointed slightly left. "Callan's in at shortstop, his favorite 'I love Derek Jeter' position."

"Well, who doesn't love the Captain?" Kimberly exchanged high fives with Tee because not loving the Yankees didn't happen in their branch of the Gallaghers. "The guy rocks."

"Mom, I'm going over to the playground to see Sophie and Reese, okay?"

"Yes, but you should have worn your sneakers. Flip-flops aren't meant for climbing."

"Sorry!"

She dashed off. Corinne followed her with her gaze, then said, "Watch."

Kimberly kept her eye on Tee as she paused at the edge of the playground, kicked off her flip-flops and began to climb like a monkey. "Don't you worry nonstop?"

"It would do me no good, so why bother?" Corinne asked. "Tee's her father's daughter, one hundred percent. Nothing is too high, too far or too fast. So I pray and encourage and watch her go."

Brave words from a woman who'd lost her husband because of similar personality traits. "Pretty gutsy on your part."

Corinne shrugged. "I've got little choice in the matter. You either learn to adjust or bang your head against the wall, repeatedly. I got tired of sore heads."

Kimberly wished she'd seen the common sense of that long ago.

"Besides, having Tee around is like having Dave here with me. I think God made her that way on purpose, so I wouldn't ever really be without him."

Kimberly fought back the lump in her throat. "Are you working tonight?"

Corinne shook her head. "I've got two nights off. Callan, great catch!" She hooted across the field as Callan scooped up a grounder and hurled it to first with Gold Glove accuracy.

"He's good."

Corinne sank back down. "He's amazing. They're already talking high school scouts. Our team isn't strong enough to make it to the Little League regionals, but Callan's progressing like crazy. Coach Cutler has been a huge help. Have you heard from your parents today?"

Kimberly shook her head. "We've prearranged eight o'clock phone calls. That way we're not all on pins and needles all day, waiting for an update."

"But you'll miss it if you're here."

Kimberly shoulder-nudged her. "Rory's there, and maybe Emily, too. If there was an emergency, they'd call me. Mom and Dad know I've got other important stuff to do. Like cheer for my nephew. And pray my niece doesn't fall off that monkey bar setup. Do you see how high that is, Corinne?"

"I do. I'm ignoring it."

"I'd be a lousy mother." Kim frowned across the ball field to where the girls raced, played and climbed around the big playground. "Overprotective and overbearing. If I have kids, they'll most likely need counseling early on. I can't look." She turned her back on the playground, determined not to witness Tee's probable annihilation.

The woman sitting in front of Kimberly turned. "I was like that. Crazy overprotective. And then my husband gave me this long lecture about letting kids be kids, about the old days, how kids have survived for countless millennia. I finally stopped worrying just to make him stop talking."

"Did it work?" Kim wondered, laughing.

"It helped." The woman stuck out her hand. "Rilla Gunther. My son's playing right field."

"Kimberly Gallagher. Crazy aunt, unaccustomed to kids."

"We'll take care of that now that you're back home." Corinne handed over a tub of popcorn. "Save me from myself. Eat some of this."

"I can't." Kimberly grimaced. "Drew bought me a monster banana split for supper at Stan's. I'm going to be stuffed for a while."

"How is Drew?" Corinne turned more directly

her way as the teams changed up at the bottom of the inning. "Better, I hope?"

Better than what? Kimberly had no idea. "He seems all right. Kind of."

Corinne frowned. "He had a rough couple of years before he left here."

"Like you didn't?" Kimberly couldn't believe she was hearing correctly. "Not to rehash old news, but being a pregnant widow with a toddler wasn't exactly a walk in the park."

"But I had them." Corinne smiled softly at the field, then the playground. "I had a part of Dave that lived on, regardless. And I was so busy that I didn't have time to be overwhelmed. And time went on. But Drew took it all on his shoulders, bore the weight of the whole thing, and when it got too heavy to carry around, he left. And that felt wrong."

"He's got a kid."

"He does?" Corinne's expression went from surprise to approval. "Good."

"She's amazing. Spunky. A mind of her own. And so funny, that same dry humor from her father. She and Tee would hit it off, and they're only a year apart. It's like female versions of Dave and Drew, all over again."

"I can't wait to meet her." Corinne raised her hand to shield her eyes from the angled sun as she looked west. "Isn't that Drew over there? Just walking in?"

Kimberly pretended her heart didn't do an adrenaline-laced gymnastic move just because Drew and Amy showed up at the town baseball game. He scanned the crowd, saw her and smiled, but when he realized she was next to Corinne, his smile faltered.

Corinne was up and off her bleacher seat in a heartbeat. She charged down the stairs, across the grass and caught Drew in a hug so big that Kimberly was pretty sure she'd bowl him over.

She didn't, but even from this distance, she read the emotion in his face as they talked. Corinne greeted Amy, pointed out the playground, and then the two adults skirted the field to introduce Amy to the growing group of kids playing there.

By the time they got back to the bleachers, the teams had changed up twice, and Callan was just coming to bat. Corinne took her seat on Kimberly's left. Drew sat on her right. When they announced Callan's name, Drew's expression tightened.

Was he seeing Dave out there? Was he remembering countless games for two of Grace Haven's best and brightest ball players? Or was he seeing that wretched, cold, fateful night?

"Watch, Drew." Corinne reached across Kimberly to pat Drew's knee. "See how he swings the bat, the way he moves, just as if you and Dave taught him. He's a natural, but unlike his father, who was kind of a slob around the house, Callan's got a place for everything and everything in its place. Which is refreshing because Tee got every bit of Dave's no-holds-barred personality."

Drew glanced sideways. "Including the messiness?"

"Exponentially worse."

"That's funny."

"It is, right?" The smile Corinne sent him was like a benediction. "It's like God did a little fun mix-up with both of them to show me just how well Dave and I did together. A good balance."

Drew started to look uncomfortable, but Corinne reached across Kimberly again and smacked him. Not hard, but hard enough to get his attention. "We count the blessings. Not the heartaches. Get with the program, Slade."

Kimberly wasn't sure what to expect. Oh, she knew how the old Drew would have reacted. He'd have agreed completely.

But this older, more somber edition seemed to carry a heavy burden. To her surprise and delight, he laughed. Then he clutched his arm, feigning injury. "I thought you were nice. What's happened to you?"

"I am nice." Corinne shot him a self-assured look. "But now I'm nice and tough. So don't think I'm going to let you get away with any moping or guilt or nonsense like that, my friend. We've finally got you back in town, and I'm going to celebrate the moral victory in that."

"How so?" Kimberly wondered.

"Well, by thanking God, of course. And taking the kids for pizza after the game. There was no time to eat between Tee's riding lesson and Cal's game, so food is a must. You guys should come with us. Kimberly, I know you're not hungry, but I promised Tee you'd be there, and you can't disappoint her."

She was right, so Kimberly nodded.

"And, Drew, you need to come and tell them Dave stories. Nobody does it better than you. These kids have heard so much about you, they think they know you. Don't disappoint them, or I'll go all Mama Bear on you, and that's not a pretty sight."

"You've put severe limitations on my choices."

She grinned, smug. "Welcome to small-town living. No place to hide, big guy. Callan! Yay!" She jumped up as the crack of the bat sent the ball deep into the outfield for an in-the-park home run. As Cal rounded the bases, his speed brought him into home plate two seconds before the well-thrown ball.

Callan didn't over-celebrate. He trotted into the dugout as if it was no big deal, high-fived a few players and took a seat, sure of himself, much like his father had been, back in the day.

Drew's body tensed beside her.

Was it Callan's resemblance to Dave or too many old-time buttons being pushed at once?

Maybe both. Sitting there, shoulder to shoulder, she wished she could help because she'd come face-to-face with a new reality today. She'd wasted way too much time already. She needed to take hold of the sage advice Drew gave her a long time ago when a knotted skate lace had given her conniptions. "Work from the middle and tease each knot loose, one by one. When you're done?" He'd handed back her figure skate and grabbed hold of her teenage heart. "Everything's fixed, good as new."

And what she wanted more than anything now, was for everything to be fixed. Good as new.

Chapter Five

The image of the boy, so like his father, pierced Drew's heart. He watched Callan in the dugout, saw the casual way he accepted his teammates' high fives. When Dave's son looked their way his mother gave him a big thumbs-up.

He smiled, then ducked his head.

Humble.

He got that attribute from Corinne, because no one had ever accused Drew and Dave of being meek.

A local police car pulled up alongside the gravel-lined path outside the field. A uniformed cop climbed out, waved to a few people, then ambled toward the bleachers.

"Kimber. Your buddy's here." Corinne's stage-whispered words made Kimberly cringe. "He's heading our way."

"A new friend?" Drew didn't turn toward

Kimberly. He was too busy watching the cop make a show of standing big, brave and tall as he spoke to a couple of parents.

"Hush. Both of you. There's a game to watch."

The cop looked up just then. His gaze scanned their section, but Drew recognized the practiced ruse. He was pretending to sweep the crowd, while checking out who was sitting with whom. For Kimberly? Or Corinne? Drew scanned his memory bank and this guy's face didn't click into place, which made him new in town.

The officer strode up the bleacher stairs, waited until the inning broke, then moved into the empty seats above them. He sat directly behind Drew, leaned down and touched Kimberly's shoulder. "Kim, how's your dad? Any news?"

Drew had watched her field questions about her dad throughout the day. Her current reaction was more guarded, and that gave him something else to wonder about. "Nothing new. We'll keep the station informed through Alejandro like we've been doing. That way everyone gets the same story."

"We'll hope for good news."

"And pray." Corinne tipped her bag of popcorn up to the officer. "Popcorn, Brian?"

"Thank you, no. I just happened to be driving by, saw the game and figured I'd stop in to see what was happening. Good to see our boys winning against a solid team like this. They've stepped up their play."

"They're working hard," Corinne agreed, but she didn't sound all that pleased, either. Again, Drew wondered why. "Brian, this is our friend, Drew Slade. Drew, this is Brian Reynolds. He works with Dad."

"Drew Slade?"

Drew waited as Brian weighed the name, and he saw the minute reality clicked in—that Drew was the cop with Dave the night he got killed.

"You've been gone awhile."

"Back now." Two could play this game, and Drew wasn't about to give information to anyone, even if they wore a uniform.

"Welcome home."

Corinne's smile softened the insincere greeting. "We're thrilled to have him back here at last. We get to spoil him a little."

"Lucky him."

"I'll say." Drew turned back to the game, hoping the guy would take the hint and leave because Kimberly was clearly uncomfortable with either him or the situation. Either one was enough for Drew to put an end to the conversation. "Nice meeting you, Brian."

"Yeah." The cop stood, realized he was blocking the game for the people on the top bleacher and ducked to the side. "You, too."

He almost swaggered down the stairs. When he was out of earshot, Drew poked Kimberly's arm. "What was that all about?"

"He wants Dad's job."

That wasn't the answer Drew expected. "You're kidding."

"Nope. Oh, he doesn't say it in so many words, but he's been needling Alejandro for weeks about appointing either a long-term interim or to place Dad on disability and hold a special election to vote in a replacement."

"He's either putting your father in the grave or dismissing him completely," Drew said. "I don't like either scenario." He kept his voice down, but the woman in front of them turned around.

"That's Brian for you. He's good at feathering his own nest. He may not be evil, but he's not all that nice, either. He watches out for numero uno, 24/7. And if you ask me, that's not a recipe for a good chief."

Drew agreed silently. A strong squad commander put his personal issues behind the good of the people and his command. That's why Pete Gallagher had enjoyed such a successful career. He wasn't afraid to be humble when needed and strong overall. "Has your dad been considering his options? Is there a reason this guy's after his job?"

"Dad's been focused on getting well." The

frown Kimberly shot toward the cop made Drew want to ease the furrow from her brow. He didn't. "But of course the department has to look at the big picture. Brian seems to show up all over the place, digging for information. My guess is he wants the job and he won't be afraid to go after it."

"What about Alejandro? Isn't he in the running?"

"His wife's company is supposedly moving their headquarters, so he won't be in contention if that's the case. It's a muddle because we're used to the way things are here. We don't do change all that well."

"That's a small-town truism for sure." Drew watched as Brian sauntered over to his car, looking haughty.

A too-proud cop was unapproachable. Sure, a cop should walk tall and strong. But not *above* the people. *With* the people. And that was a big difference, no matter what beat you walked.

The girls raced around the outside of the field just then. Amy's eyes were shining, and when Tee Gallagher dashed up the bleacher steps, the noise and clatter she raised said yes, this was Dave's daughter to the max.

"Tee. People are trying to watch the game. In peace, darling. Tone it down, okay?" Corinne's expression indicated they'd had this conversation many times before, and then she slanted a look at Drew, a "see what I mean?" look. And he did. He smiled, remembering.

"Sorry, Mom!" She popped into the seat behind Kimberly, Amy sat behind Drew and a third girl grabbed the seat behind Corinne. "Any popcorn left?"

Corinne sent a guilty look to the bag.

Tee groaned, and Drew stood up. "I'm on a popcorn run. You girls each want one?"

Quick affirmative answers sent him down the bleacher stairs to the sports boosters' hutch. "Can I have three popcorns, please?"

"Drew Slade, you can have as many as you like! It's so good to have you in town, and way more handsome than ever." Bertie Engle laughed to see him as her husband scooped and buttered three big round tubs of popcorn. "You're feeding that crew up top, I expect, and you're right to get the big size. Tee Gallagher can eat this in a New York minute, and I expect her friends can do likewise. How are you, Drew?" She looked right at him as if he mattered, and when he met her gaze, it felt like he mattered and that was good. "Gosh, it's nice to see you again."

"It's good to be here." He handed over a twenty. When she went to make change, he shook his head. "Put it in the fund. Equipment costs are crazy high."

"They sure are." Hi Engle nodded as he fed more kernels into the decades-old machine. "But in the end, it's worth it because we all come back to two things. God and baseball."

"Do you still play?" Bertie wondered as she handed him the first two tubs. "Or working too hard to have time?"

"The second choice."

"Well, maybe there'll be time now that you're back."

He wasn't back, but he couldn't launch an explanation to these two nice people, folks who'd supported the local baseball league and the booster club for decades. "That would be fun, Bertie."

"Oh, it would, wouldn't it?" She beamed at him, and it didn't matter that they were both older and water had flowed under a lot of bridges… Her gaze said welcome home. And meant it.

He handed out the popcorn once he got back to the bleachers. Rocky sat politely, straight and tall at his side, watching the game.

"May I pet him?" Tee wondered. She wiped her hand on her pants and ignored her mother's groan. "He's a really gorgeous dog."

"Sure." The game broke for the seventh inning stretch, and Tee and Reese took turns petting the stalwart shepherd. As the teams were preparing to take the field, Kimberly turned his way. "So you guys got settled into the B and B okay?"

"Last-minute change of plans."

Kimberly frowned. "How so?"

"The B and B isn't pet-friendly."

The furrow between her brows deepened. "They didn't want Rocky there?"

"She suggested a kennel run by the local veterinary."

"A kennel?" Corinne's brows shot up. "For a police dog? I can't imagine not allowing a service dog on the premises."

"Oh, Drew." Kimberly put her hand on his bare arm, and the soft touch of cool, long fingers scrambled his thoughts. "I'm so sorry I suggested it. I had no idea they'd have a problem with Rocky."

"They haven't given away my room at the Country Inn, so I think we'll just head over there after the game."

"That strands Amy while you're working."

He didn't see any way to help that. "Yes, but—"

Corinne leaned around Kimberly. "You're both being stupid. The garage apartment would be perfect." She pointed at Drew. "You're going to be working with Kimber, Amy would be in town and Rocky will love being at Mom and Dad's."

"The mop-dog isn't exactly one of Rocky's

fans." Drew scrambled for words because the thought of living there, with Kimberly, Emily and Rory in the big house, surrounded by reminders of Dave and all they'd lost, seemed wrong.

"Mags will adjust. This is perfect!" Corinne exclaimed. "It solves both problems and saves you a boatload of money."

"The senator pays, so—"

"Then we just made a nice contribution to his presidential campaign by saving him a solid chunk of change. It's the ideal solution, isn't it, Kimberly?"

It wasn't the least bit ideal. The thought of having Drew second-guessing everything she did with the upcoming wedding was mind-boggling enough, but to have him there, living in the carriage-house garage apartment her parents usually rented out to college kids?

"Can we do that?" Amy peeked around Kimberly's shoulder from above and met her gaze. "Would that be okay? Because I'd really love to be in town, and then Rocky wouldn't have to feel like a burden."

"Dogs don't feel like burdens," Kimberly protested, but when she looked around at the big, burly shepherd, his deep brown eyes did look a little guilt-stricken. Which meant she didn't have a choice. "Of course you can use the apartment. It probably needs a cleaning."

"Amy and I've done our share of that." Drew looked up at Amy, and she grinned, agreeing.

"We've been splitting chores for years," Amy assured her. "Can we clean it first thing in the morning? Does that work for your work schedule, Dad?"

Drew arched one eyebrow in his daughter's direction. "So all of a sudden you're worried about my work schedule? Now that you've crossed multiple states, broken a ton of rules and interrupted a very important job?"

She nodded, undeterred. "Well, sure. As long as Team Slade is together, we look out for one another. Right?"

Corinne covered her laugh with a quick cough, but Kimberly didn't bother. "Man, she's got your number, Drew."

He didn't argue. "That she does. You're sure you don't mind, Kimberly? None of this is going according to how your mother and Shelby arranged things. I never intended that my job here would put you on the spot like this."

Kimberly hadn't planned on any of this, either, but compared with what her father was going through, her life was a cakewalk. "I think it's a great solution, actually. Rocky won't be displaced, Amy will love being in town and within walking distance to the office—"

"And Stan's," she broke in, grinning.

"The money we save in lodging costs could be lost in ice-cream consumption," Drew noted. He turned and looked straight at Kimberly, and she had to clamp down her racing heart when he did. "You're okay with this? Really?"

What had she just pondered in the car on the way to the game? That she and Drew had fallen behind the times because of their enforced hiatus away from town, family and friends. Maybe this was life's way of working things out, finally. "I'm fine with it."

"Then it's a done deal."

Amy screeched and high-fived Tee and Reese.

The game ground to an end about fifteen minutes later. The Grace Haven Indians lost by one, and it was a glum home team that headed to parked cars after a meeting with the coach.

"Nice game, Cal." Corinne clapped a hand on his shoulder, and Drew was surprised to see how tall the boy was up close. Not looking him in the eye yet, but he had a good four inches on his mother. "Cal, this is your godfather. Drew Slade."

Her words startled the boy. He stood still, then squared his shoulders and stared up into Drew's eyes, and if anger and distrust had a look, it was reflected in Callan Gallagher's gaze. "You were my dad's friend."

"Yes." Drew met the hard gaze and refused to back down.

"And my godfather?"

A position he'd abdicated by leaving town and not making contact after Dave died. "Yes."

"And you were my dad's partner the night he was killed." The boy didn't ask the question; he made it a statement of fact.

"Callan." Corinne stepped in to stop him, but Drew shook his head.

"Let him have his say, Corinne."

The boy's smirk said Drew wasn't worth wasting too many words on, and his rudc cxpression made Kimberly want to jump in and defend Drew—which was a sudden turnaround. "I don't have anything more to say. I think what you did speaks for itself. I'll be in the car, Mom."

He strode off, his athletic bag banging against his leg, head down.

"Drew, I'm sorry." Corinne moved around in front of Drew and put her hands on his upper arms. "I know that's hurtful, and I know he's being a brat, but—"

Drew shook his head. "He's stating an opinion, Corinne. One that's been fostered by ten years of being ignored by his godfather and not having a father around. I screwed up, big-time, but now that I'm here for a while, maybe I can make some of it up to him. I'd like a chance to try."

"You don't mind?" Corinne waved a hand toward the parked car. "Because I think it would be good for him to get to know you, too."

"Once he moves beyond the death-ray, kill-you-with-his-eyes stage," Kimberly added. "From the look of things, that might take a while."

"You're not helping," Corinne scolded, but Kimberly saw Drew's gaze lighten slightly, and knew he understood.

"Drew and Dave were intense, just like Callan," she noted as they walked toward the parking lot. "And boneheaded, to boot. They've got a lot in common, so my vote is yes. Drew should see if he can mend some old fences while he's here."

"Kimberly Gallagher, grief counselor?" Drew raised a brow her way as she moved toward her car.

She shook her head. "Nah, just Kimberly who's made the same mistakes you have. And figures there's no time like the present to see if we can smooth things over. So while you're trying to make amends with my grumpy nephew, I'm going to see if I can smooth the ruffled feathers of my two sisters because the last thing either of them wanted was to have me bust in here and take over. In some ways it needed to happen. But that doesn't make it a comfortable situation."

"We can compare notes on a nightly basis," Drew told her as he opened the back door of the SUV for Rocky. "Because I'm not opposed to taking advice."

"Does that mean you're going to advise me on how to handle Emily and Rory?"

He cringed. "Maybe."

The fear on his face suggested he understood what she didn't dare say. The three sisters loved each other in absentia, but thrown together they made a volatile mix, like a high school chemistry session gone amok. And Kimberly's mother had started adding to the tension by confiding in Kimberly on the side. That made the evolving sister relationship trickier.

He turned back her way before he got into his car. "I might not be a lot of help, Kimber. But I'll do my best."

She couldn't ask for more than that. "Me, too. Come by in the morning, and we'll get you guys settled into that apartment, okay?"

"We'll be there first thing. Then I'll buy you breakfast. Or lunch if you're not a breakfast eater. And we can set up a staging area for the wedding consultations."

"Agreed." She climbed into the car and didn't dare try to sort through the mix of emotions. Hers, Drew's, Callan's, Amy's, Corinne's... Only Tee seemed delightfully unaffected by the drama, and that reaction was twofold. First, she hadn't been born when her dad died, so she never had a relationship to lose. And, second, she was her father's daughter, and Dave would be the last person to hold a grudge or carry deadweight.

Dave spoke his mind and moved on, and if she'd just taken a few minutes to talk with him after that final phone call...but she hadn't. She'd acted like a first-class jerk—and then Dave was gone.

Her phone buzzed. She answered as she pulled into the shaded yard of her parents' home. "Hey, Mom. How's everything going?"

"Not as well as I let your sisters believe, I'm afraid."

That meant her mother had painted things optimistically when she'd called the home phone at eight o'clock. "Mom, we can't shade the truth with them. You've got to be honest."

"I was, mostly. But Emily's had such a rough year, and Rory takes things so seriously. You're the strong one, Kimber."

Kimberly appreciated the compliment, but she saw both sides. Her sisters would be justifiably angry to be babied about something this crucial.

"Mom, Dad's prognosis isn't the kind of thing you try to pretty up. We all need to go into this with our eyes wide-open. This is important stuff, and everyone realizes that. It's not fair to hide things from them."

"I'm not hiding anything," Kate retorted. "I'm taking an optimistic point of view, but I need someone to be honest with. And that's you, kiddo. Like it or not, you're in the driver's seat right now. It's better to ease into all of this, especially with the additional workload my absence has put on everyone. How are the plans for the Vandeveld wedding going? Signed, sealed and delivered?"

Now it was Kimberly who painted a brighter picture. "We've had to make adjustments to fit the new security profile because Shelby's dad is the party candidate, but we got it done and we're filling in the blanks."

"Such as?"

"Simple things." Kimberly fudged the answer. If Kate realized they'd changed everything about the wedding at this late date, she'd worry, and she didn't need more worry on her plate. Was she acting just like her mother? Kind of. "We've got it covered."

"And Drew is there?"

"Yes, much to my surprise. You knew he

was heading the security detail and you kept it to yourself."

"Because I love you both," her mother acknowledged. "I decided it was time for you to get over blaming him for what happened to your brother. Every cop's family knows that sometimes things happen. We can't live life by what-ifs. It's not healthy."

"I agree."

"Really?" Her mother's voice pitched up in approval. "That's good to hear. They've redone all the tests and blood work your dad just endured up there to find out the exact same thing they already knew, and I have to say that's really frustrating him. We'll be in to see the doctor who does the laser ablation soon, and I can't deny I'm scared."

"You're never afraid of anything, Mom. And you raised us the same way."

"I've never had to face a condition like this before," her mother confessed. "I'm putting on a good face for your sisters and the station house, but this treatment is too new for any real prognosis. It's like I'm risking your father's life and I'm not a big risk taker by nature."

That was true. "But every successful treatment starts somewhere. This time it starts with us."

"You think so?"

"Why not? I've looked at the online research. These guys have science and technology on their side."

"Let us then approach God's throne of grace with confidence." Kate quoted the shortened line from Hebrews softly. "Kimberly, you're absolutely right."

Kim wasn't sure how she tied in with the biblical passage because she'd been thinking along more pragmatic lines of man fixing man via education, but if quoting scripture helped her mother deal with this crisis, then so be it. "I love being right."

"Listen, I've got to go, but if you could run interference for me, I'd be grateful."

"With Em and Rory? Or the acting chief of police? Or the whole town?"

"All of the above, and thank you!"

"Mom, I—"

"They're bringing Dad down the hall, honey. I must run."

The phone disconnected.

Kimberly climbed out of the car as Mags dashed out the back door, barking, flying across the grass in a series of leaps and bounds, happy to welcome her home.

She scooped up Mags, accepted a few quick dog kisses to her cheek, then pointed to the garage behind them. "Tomorrow, you and I are going to start a new normal. Rocky and Drew are going to be underfoot, and we both need to behave. We have to be accepting. And more open to change. Got it?"

The Yorkie's expression looked doubtful, but when she pressed another quick kiss to Kimberly's cheek, Kim took it as a doggie version of "I'll try."

And then she hoped she was right.

Chapter Six

"You told Drew he could use the garage apartment without checking with us?" Emily stared at the coffeemaker for long, slow seconds before facing Kimberly in the morning. "You didn't think that might inconvenience anyone? What if we'd promised it to a college kid? The new semester starts in two weeks."

"Leave me out of this." Hands up, Rory took a firm step back. "I think it's a great idea. Drew's kid gets to be in town. She's going to help me out in the mornings, and if she's living in the backyard, I can just grab her and head to work. It works for me."

"I'm not saying it's a bad idea." Emily's frown deepened. For a former beauty queen, she really should know better. Maybe Kimberly should buy her some anti-wrinkle cream. Then again, considering the mutinous look on her sister's face right now, maybe not.

"I would have appreciated being consulted. That's all I'm saying."

Kimberly bit back a large dose of pride and nodded. "You're right, of course. I'm used to making decisions on my own. I should have called and asked last night. Corinne made the suggestion and I jumped on it. I felt bad about sending Drew to the B and B and having them refuse to let Rocky stay. Aside from the surprise factor, do either of you have a problem with it?"

"Not me." Rory pulled a loaf of fresh bread out of the bread drawer. "Anybody want toast? I've got to fly soon. Tell Amy I'll have her help me tomorrow if she wants to help clean the apartment today."

"Sure. Em?" Kimberly turned back toward Emily and raised her diplomacy level a notch. "Is it all right with you?"

Emily scowled, then shrugged. "It's too late now, so what's the point of asking?"

True, but… "Because if we need to make different arrangements, we can. I should have asked first. My bad."

"It's fine, Kimberly. Just—" Emily shrugged one shoulder again, grabbed her coffee and headed out the door. "Do what you want."

The wooden screen door banged shut.

Kimberly picked up her mug and sank into a chair opposite Rory. "That went well." She sent the youngest Gallagher a rueful look. "I didn't mean to upset her."

"You didn't. Life did. The two of you are like high-speed commuter trains coming from opposite directions on a single track. My guess is we're in for multiple mishaps until the pecking order is established."

"There doesn't have to be a pecking order," Kimberly argued, "because I'm only here for as long as it takes to help Mom and Dad. Then you can be rid of me again."

"No one wants to be rid of you, and I'd love to have us all back together," Rory scolded. "Mom and Dad would love that, too."

"This coming from the woman who's planning a mission trip next year."

Rory grinned and shrugged. "That's a temporary move, not a permanent relocation. But you're wrong about the pecking order thing. Mom made it clear that you were the Gallagher in charge when it came to Kate & Company."

"But it's not like Emily wants the business. Or does she? Is she thinking of staying here and working with Mom?"

Rory buttered her toast and took a bite. "No. Maybe. I don't know. All I know is that the two of you have each had a rough time. Her scoundrel husband dumped her—your fiancé dumped you. Emily's out of a job because she worked for her husband's family business, and you're out of a job because of restructuring. Neither of you did anything wrong, but here you are. One business…three sisters." She pointed to herself. "One of whom thinks the wedding industry is about the most overrated, pumped-up drain on family finances known to man, so the race is on between you two. I will happily move off to do mission work in emerging nations and watch folks jump the broom. The outlay of money I see go through accounts for these weddings could feed a lot of people around the world."

"Do you think Mom's right?"

Rory looked puzzled. "About?"

"Life. Love. Circumstance. I was let go on a personal and professional level just in time to come here and help out. Same with Emily. Do you think that's a God thing or just a coincidence?"

Rory answered as she put together a sack of peanut butter and jelly sandwiches to share with her preschoolers. "It's always a God thing, sis. I've got no doubt of that. And to have both of you back here in time to help save Mom's business at the very time Dad was diagnosed is huge. So my vote goes to God, absolutely. But while He gives us the means to help, He expects us to do the work involved."

"Which means being more sensitive to Emily's feelings."

"Yes. And the same for her. You two always butted heads. And you haven't had to live together in a long time."

"I do get bossy. She probably hates that," Kimberly admitted.

"Can't blame her there."

The sound of Drew's voice brought Kimberly's head around. "You're early."

"Strategic maneuver. That way I get to overhear snippets of what's up and what's going down." He stepped in, and the minute he did, Mags mad-dashed through the house, warning the world of the intruder in their midst. Whcn she got to Drew she pulled up tight, sat her bottom down and panted up at him, tail wagging against the hardwood floor.

"She likes you?" Kimberly sent the dog a look of wonder. "What's up with that, Mags? Yesterday you were ready to eat him alive—"

One deep, loud *woof* sounded outside.

Mags ignored Drew and leaped for the screen door. It hadn't latched tightly when Drew came in. It gave way just enough for the miniature spitfire to charge through, across the pillared porch and down the steps. Mags's furious barking sounded as if she meant business.

Drew hurried through the door, followed by Kimberly and Rory.

Taut, the two dogs stood, staring, a classic face-off, the barrel-chested shepherd on the right, the silky-haired terrier on the left. Mags began to circle, as if sizing up Rocky's weak spots, except the beautiful big shepherd had no weak spots, and while he stood his ground, his expression said Mags was a nuisance. Nothing more.

And that indifference only seemed to incite the little puffball further.

"Mags! Come here."

Mags did nothing of the sort.

"Magnolia Blossom Gallagher, get over here." Rory's use of the dog's full name accomplished little.

Drew knelt down, one hand out, and chirruped to the little dog.

She turned, ears up, saw him at her level and flew across the grass to him. She yapped a little, just enough to explain her concerns about big dogs and territorial rights. Drew nodded as he picked her up, murmuring soft sounds of doggie understanding.

Kimberly's heart went into full crunch mode.

He could have been annoyed that their spoiled

purse-dog was pestering a trained K-9 partner. He could have been angry. He could have scolded the little dog for being a pain-in-the-neck ankle biter, but he didn't, and his gentleness worked on the dog…

And on Kimberly.

"Patience." She reminded herself as she moved closer to Drew's side. "Why do I always forget that part?"

Drew's understanding smile made her feel better. "Getting down to their level can break the standoff."

"A ploy you might want to use with Emily, Kimber." Rory grinned and called for Amy. "Kid, are you coming with me or staying here and cleaning?"

Amy had been checking things out around the garage and the sorely neglected gardens. Kate Gallagher would cry to see her gardens in such a state, but none of the girls had found time to dig, weed, spray or transplant. With fall drawing near, the days were growing shorter. She came their way and looked up at Drew. "Do you care if I go help Rory? Or would you rather I stay and help you guys clean?"

Drew consulted Kimberly with a raised brow. "Your call."

"Go with Rory," she decided, and she smiled when Rory's face lit up. "Your dad and I can handle this in a couple of hours. And then we'll move right into setting up the planning station for Shelby's wedding, okay?"

"Works for me." He gave Amy a big hug and a kiss. "Don't make the little kids too crazy, okay? And don't wander away. And follow Rory's directions. And don't be a pain."

She laughed and hugged him around the waist, clearly happy to be here, with him. "I'm going to be absolutely perfect, Dad. No worries."

"Ha. Right." He tweaked her nose and smiled as they walked toward Rory's car. When they had backed out of the driveway, he turned toward Kimberly. "She won't be perfect, which is okay because I like her just the way she is. I passed Emily on her way to the office this morning, and she wasn't looking any too happy. Did you two go at it?"

"We did not 'go at' anything." Kimberly went back into the kitchen to gather cleaning supplies, and if she thrust the wash bucket at Drew with a little more force than necessary, it was probably an accident. Or not.

He laughed, but then he sobered. "Your mother told me that Emily's husband walked out on their marriage and left her without a job. Maybe you two could find common ground."

"Because neither one of us can hold a man's

attention or a position. Maybe we can start a support group. Losers-R-Us."

His frown said she was being absurd, and, since he was right, she sighed and started again. "We should, but it's never been easy between Emily and me. We're the water and oil, the constant clash. Rory's the calm, caring one. The equalizer. Maybe if Emily and I were more alike—"

"More alike would be dangerous to society as we know it."

"You are beyond mistaken." She put the key in the apartment door lock, wiggled the handle just so and unlocked the door. "We're nothing alike."

His silence hinted that she was wrong, but what did he know about it? He was an only child who didn't have to deal with siblings.

Kimberly had held a job at a local store since she was fifteen, and had helped her mother besides. Going to a local college had offered her more time in Kate & Company, so when she graduated with her business and project management degree, stepping into the big world of country music and Nashville complemented her hard work.

Emily had secured a college scholarship through beauty pageant wins. She'd graduated, gone on to become Miss New York, met Christopher Barrister, won his heart and a job in the buying offices of the great Barrister's Department Store chain without doing much more than looking drop-dead gorgeous in a bikini. Until he'd walked out of their marriage last winter, citing the marriage...*and Emily*...as a mistake.

Drew was right; they did have stuff in common. But Kimberly had worked her way up every rung of the ladder.

Emily flashed smiles and looked pretty, which meant they really didn't have much in common after all. And yet...they needed to find common ground, for their parents' sake, especially now.

"I haven't been in this apartment since I was a kid." Drew's observation made a welcome change of subject. "Dave and I used to pretend we were spies. We'd watch for enemies coming into the harbor."

"And shoot them with your ray guns?"

He looked appalled. "Light sabers, Kimber. Get with the program."

"Stalking the evil empire."

"Now you're talkin'." He rolled up his sleeves.

And Kimberly put a firm grip on her appreciation. *You will not notice his great arms, and the nice tan he's acquired. Avert your gaze!*

"How about if I vacuum first, and then we dust and wash things down?"

"You do your own cleaning?" She took the bottle of spray cleaner and a wet washcloth over to the small bank of kitchen cabinets and pointed behind him to a small closet. “Vacuum's in there. No maid service at your place? I'm kind of surprised.”

“Nah.” He moved to the closet, opened the door and pulled out the small cleaner. “It's just the two of us. I travel light and the kid's unusually neat, which means fewer parent battles and more discretionary funding.”

“Double win.” She pulled a chair over to reach the uppermost shelves and climbed up, “I don't know when this got cleaned last, so if I come across any weird little creatures and scream like a girl, pay me no mind. Unless I keep screaming, in which casc it's all right to comc running.”

He would, too. Standing there, watching her climb onto the chair, he visualized running to save her.

He'd haul her down off the chair, set her safely on the old linoleum floor and then…

He wouldn't let himself get to “then,” because there couldn't be a then. There was barely a “now,” and that was only because they'd quietly agreed to work together.

And now you're going to live about sixty feet apart. Might be time to restrategize your plans, because having Kimberly around day and night isn't going to be easy on either of you.

He'd make it easy because the Gallaghers were facing tough times. Maybe God had sent him on this job to bring some sort of reconciliation to a family he'd hurt years ago.

Dave's death wasn't his fault. He understood that.

But it had happened on *his* watch, which meant if he could bring peace and strength to the Gallaghers, he was doing God's work. And that he could handle. He finished vacuuming the two small bedrooms and the braided rug in the living area before Kimberly completed the cabinets. "Slowpoke."

She made a face and flicked water at him.

"Don't start something you can't finish," he warned. Eyes down, he pulled out a can of spray polish and a dust cloth.

More water flicked his way.

He turned, picked up the kitchen sink sprayer, turned the cool water on and gave her a quick spray.

She screeched, and he was just about to remind her she'd been forewarned, when she screeched again, pointing.

A half-dollar-size black spider scurried out of the far corner of the cupboard, clearly disoriented by the light, the noise and the activity. Kimberly went to step back, missed the edge of the chair and started to tumble.

Except Drew caught her.

Wide blue eyes looked up at him. Beautiful eyes. Searching. Wondering.

He was wondering, too, but one of them had strict rules of engagement and a spider to kill, so he tweaked her nose, climbed up on the chair and dispatched the furry beast quickly. When he tossed away the paper towel, Kimberly put a hand to her heart, making light of the situation. "My hero."

"At your service, ma'am. And I didn't even have to draw my weapon."

"You employed hand-to-hand combat." She pulled the chair to the next cupboard and smiled up at him. "Well played."

"Rescuing a beautiful woman isn't a hardship, Kimber. Not in this case, anyway."

He shouldn't have added that last, but he couldn't help himself, and when she pivoted to face him, he recognized the look in her gaze. Longing, like him. Interested, like him. They'd been thrust together for a few weeks of work. Their paths would diverge at the end of September. He'd be in Jersey and Manhattan; she'd be here, helping her parents.

Bad timing or good? He didn't know, but he broke the look and went back to dusting. "Call me if you come under attack again. I've got a weapon in hand." He held up the dust cloth. "And I'm not afraid to use it."

"Will do."

As they finished, she checked her watch and winced. "Listen, I need to clean up before I go to the office. Can we do a working lunch a little later? And do you mind grabbing the food? I've got a noon appointment with Emily and a new wedding client. She's taking lead, but I'm advising, so I have to be there. I can't do a client intake meeting when I smell like industrial-strength cleaner."

"Can do." Drew reached out and brushed a fleck of something from the curve of her cheek. "Hold still. There. Got it."

She made a face. "Should I ask what it was? Or better off not knowing?"

"We'll call it an unknown entity and leave it at that," Drew decided. He gathered up the paper towels and the bathroom cleaning supplies as Kimberly filled Drew in on his new living arrangements. "There's no Wi-Fi out here, but there is in the house. I'll get you the password so you can use your computer. And can you make lunch at one-thirty? Just in case we run over. This is an unusual circumstance wedding. The bride and groom are both deployed, and we're trying to plan the wedding around their return this winter."

"Winters here are nothing to take lightly. There's little reprieve, and it's a rough time for weddings."

"You're right, and this will be my first northern winter in a bunch of years. I'm hoping I can man up and be brave. I might have lost my heartiness down south."

"I don't think you've lost a thing, Kimber." He put the last of the cleaning supplies back into the box and carried it down the stairs. He didn't look back to see her face. "I think your parents are blessed to have you here, your sisters are grateful for your help and expertise, and Mags will love you for all time, no matter what winter brings."

He stopped when he realized she wasn't walking behind him. He turned, then stopped, dismayed. "I made you cry?"

"Shut up." She swiped her fists against her cheeks much like she'd done as a tough-as-nails kid. The sight inspired a wealth of old feelings. Friendship, grace, family, fun and love. He'd had it all at the Gallagher house.

"Come on—stop. I was just being nice. I didn't mean a word of it. Just ignore me, I should have just been quiet." He pretended dismay, trying to tease her out of the funk of emotions, and when she laughed, he hoped his ploy was working. "Did you seriously get all worked up because I called you a blessing? Because that's preposterous behavior. You should know how amazing you are, and always have been, and not be surprised when someone mentions it. Next time just say thank you and be done with it."

"You're bossing me around again. What's up with you, Drew Slade? One minute you're all nice and sweet, and the next you're ordering me around like one of your lackeys, which I'm not, by the way."

"Oh, I get that." He grinned down at her and swept one last stray tear from her cheek. "But it made you stop bawling, didn't it?"

"I wasn't bawling. I was…emotional."

He slung an arm around her shoulders and headed toward the house. "Right. We can call it that for the moment, but I know what I saw. You're a softie, Kimber. You just don't want anyone to know it."

Chapter Seven

She didn't want anyone to know it, especially him, so why did she fall apart because he was nice, and kind, and sweet, and good?

She cleaned up and avoided Drew by slipping out the back door, into the bright summer sun, then made it to the office minutes before Emily's client was scheduled.

"I was afraid you'd forgotten." Emily had set the office chairs in a semicircle so they could converse without a desk between them once the client arrived.

"The housecleaning was a little more intense than anticipated, but it's done now, I'm clean and I'm here. Do we have cream and sugar for the coffee set up?"

Emily pointed to the far side of the coffee brewing system. "I just put them out. And brochures from all the wedding partners."

"Good. The trick to partnering with outside businesses is to make sure the bride loves what the recommended business offers. If they settle for the partnership because they're saving ten or fifteen percent, you generally end up with problems because they *feel* like they've settled. And that's never good. Weddings generate enough problems without any help from us."

"When we're done here, will you go over the regatta scheduling with me?"

Emily extended the request like a white flag of surrender, and Kimberly knew she needed to be more sensitive to her sister's needs. Em was a survivor, like her. Being thrust back into the family nest, even for good reason, was a tough pill to swallow. "Sure. Drew's grabbing lunch in about ninety minutes and bringing it over. You hungry?"

"I will be then."

The common sense of Em's answer made Kimberly smile. "How about you, Allison?"

Allison shook her head as she rearranged a seating chart for an upcoming wedding on the wall-mounted planning board. "Thanks, but no. I brown-bagged today. We're saving for our winter break trip with the kids, and every dollar we save goes into a bank shaped like a princess castle."

"Remember when we did that, Kimber?" Emily looked up from the computer as she started a new file for the incoming client. "Mom and Dad saved money for two years to land us that vacation."

"And then Dave got the stomach bug, and they had to take turns staying at the hotel with him—"

"While the other parent took three girls to the theme park."

"And on roller coasters."

"And Mom hated roller coasters."

"But Dad loved them."

Emily sighed, then smiled at Allison. "You'll have a ball, no matter what. I loved that vacation."

"Me, too." Kimberly swiped a smudge off the tabletop, recalling that week. All of them together, and poor David. So sick for the first two days.

"You didn't even want to go, remember?" Emily's expression said one of them had a faulty memory and it wasn't her. "You were in love with Cory Albemarle and his jump shot on the basketball courts. You even tried out for cheerleading."

"Oh, I remember. I didn't make the squad, and Cory asked you out instead."

"Did he?" Emily frowned. "Did I say yes? Because I don't ever remember going out with Cory Albemarle."

"You refused because you knew I liked him."

Emily's brows shot up. "I was nice to you?"

"That once." Kimberly angled Emily a teasing look. "Yes, you were nice. Very nice because I was heartbroken for days. Was that really seventeen years ago? We could use another dose about now, don't you think?"

She wasn't sure if Em would laugh or lambaste her. Laughter won and Kimberly smiled, relieved. "What did I see in him?"

"He was second fiddle to Drew Slade, so you thought you could trade down. Didn't work out so well."

Emily knew she liked Drew way back then? She turned, surprised, but Emily sent her a sister-to-sister look. "You think I didn't know you were crushing on Drew? You had his name written all over the inside cover of your high school freshman agenda. With a hot-pink heart border."

"A folder that was in my binder backward so no one could see," Kimberly reminded her. "You snooped in my private folder?"

Emily cringed as the phone rang. "Possibly. But I think the statute of limitations is up on that particular crime. Or maybe I just hope it is." She answered the phone, expressed regret to the caller, then began leafing through the early September schedule.

Kimberly knew the signs. Their noon appointment was a no-show.

Mental red flags popped up. Missing your initial appointment with a wedding planner didn't ingratiate clients. Time was money, and unless he had a really good excuse, canceling five minutes before the scheduled appointment was really bad form. "He's not coming."

Emily disconnected the call as she nodded. "Sick kid. I could hear her crying in the background. She sounded inconsolable. I rescheduled him for later in September."

"Won't that limit the choices?" Kimberly asked.

"A winter wedding does that by way of being a winter wedding," Emily reminded her. "We'll still have plenty of time to put the actual wedding together. There's no problem arranging for a hall or inn or party house in February. And where will we be in February, Kimber?"

Kimberly took the chair facing Emily and pondered the question. "Who knows? What will Dad's status be? Will we be needed here?" She tapped her mouth with the index finger of her left hand, an ingrained habit. "Right now I won't let myself think past Christmas. Keep things going here, get Dad home and celebrate the holidays at the end of the year. And then face the future."

"Well, that's months away, so we've got time." Emily leaned forward. "Are you as scared as I am?"

"Yes."

"Oh, good." Emily's wry smile said she was hoping for that answer.

"I hate that Mom's there alone, but there's not much we can do about that during the busy season. If we left the office shorthanded to be with them, she'd be frantic."

"I know. I've thought of that, often."

"But I hate that they're so far away, alone, struggling through this," Kimberly added.

"Isn't that part of the whole wedding vow thing?" Allison shot them a look over her shoulder as she finished arranging name cards for the final three tables of an ornate reception layout. "Sickness and health? For richer, for poorer? They're living their vows right now. And that's a good thing."

"She's right, although I'm somewhat jaded about the whole vow thing these days." Emily pulled up her spreadsheet on the upcoming September regatta. "Come look at this and see if there's anything I missed."

Kimberly pointed at the itinerary almost instantly. "You need to allow more time for the speeches. A lot of these people get long-winded when they're in front of their yacht-club friends.

And then here, where you've got the dinner plan? Make sure your vegetarian entrée is organic. They may sneak into the lounge and eat three chocolate bars for dessert..."

"Or take uneaten desserts off of other tables." Allison laughed. "Hey, Drew."

Kimberly turned and glanced at the clock.

"I'm early because I was done with my work and figured Allison could show me which room we're using for the staging area." Drew scanned the office. "Where's your client?"

"Home with a sick kid."

He frowned. "That's never fun. So what's wrong with the dessert-snatching scenario? Why waste good desserts? That's wrong on multiple counts. I may have saved a few forgotten desserts from the Dumpster in my time."

"Waste not, want not."

He smiled in full agreement. "Absolutely. Point me in the right direction, Kimber, and I'll get out of your hair."

She didn't want him out of her hair, or even really, out of sight, and that could become a problem. Maybe it already was and it was only day two. "We're going to use the dungeon."

"There really is one? I'm intrigued."

She hooked a thumb. "Come see."

She ignored the elevator and took the stairs to the subterranean level. Drew whistled lightly as she unlocked a door to a walled-in office, no windows, no access, other than through the fire door. "Mom always has a contingency plan, and she kept this room to be used as a backup office in case the upstairs ever got damaged by storm, fire, whatever."

"This is a small fortress."

"Perfect for our current needs, right?"

"Can I change the lock on the door?"

She understood the gravity of keeping Shelby's wedding plans confidential and nodded. "Both doors. Just leave us keys once this is done, okay?"

"If I forget to leave them, it gives me reason to come back."

He was looking down when he said it, matter-of-fact, and when he angled his gaze up to her, her heart tripped and fell a little more. "Or you could just come back, Drew. Without a contrived reason. There's no law against that."

He frowned as he went over the wiring and internet cable connections. "The thought of hurting Dave's kid more might be reason enough for me to stay away, Kimber." His expression didn't change. His voice did. "I never thought about it from Callan's point of view until he let me have it last night."

"He's a kid. They tend to have mono-vision."

"He was right," Drew corrected her. He made

a couple of notes on a pad of paper, then took a step back, surveying the room as he spoke. "He lost his father, and his godfather stayed away out of guilt, so that made all those baptismal pledges a whole lot of hot air on my part."

"You're here now."

He looked up, thoughtful. "You don't think it's a stupid idea? To try and make things better?"

"Better can't possibly be stupid." She met his gaze. "Breaking down barriers might not be easy. But it's a good mental health exercise."

"I should talk to Corinne again."

"She'll agree because she's the most sensible, hardworking person I know. And she must hate that Callan's holding this grudge."

"He's not the only one that's blamed me, Kimber."

He meant her, of course. Knowing that, she shifted her gaze. "I needed someone to blame, Drew. You were handy. It was unfair, and I'm sorry."

"Me, too."

She glanced back his way. He was watching her, hands by his side, letting her take the lead, but she couldn't quite do that yet so she glanced around the room. "So this will work?"

"It's stellar." His phone buzzed. He checked the display and texted someone quickly. "Daryl's upstairs. I'm going to keep this off-limits for Amy, okay? On a need-to-know basis. The less she knows, the tighter the security."

"Understood. We can have her working upstairs in the afternoons."

"And I'll try to schedule anything we need to do down here for the a.m. That way she doesn't notice us disappearing downstairs."

"Are you afraid she'll talk?"

He straightened his shoulders and shook his head. "If this wedding gets targeted by anyone with mal intent, getting a kid hostage is a great way of ferreting information."

"You're serious."

"Always. I do believe I've mentioned that before."

"I thought you were being overly dramatic."

"Not when it comes to safety." His grave expression underscored his words.

"Not to change the subject, but did you order lunch?"

He laughed and nodded. "Yes. Josie's delivering it probably right about now."

"So let's eat and then you, me, Rocky and Daryl can go over the routes we need to have ready, which will be much easier now with the simplified location."

"Perfect. You give me the bridal perspective of what could go wrong from points A to B, and then Daryl and I will examine from a security vantage point."

That made sense. Brides could be unpredictable creatures. And while Shelby seemed like a sensible woman, Kimberly understood the vagaries of wedding-day stress. Her job was to make sure that wedding-day jitters didn't put anyone in harm's way.

They locked up the basement office, took the back door out of the building and came around the front just as Rory arrived with Amy. "Dad! I had the best morning! Oh, my gosh, you should see all the fun things Rory let me do with the kids! It was wonderful! I felt like I never wanted to leave."

Drew didn't miss his daughter's latest hint that she loved Grace Haven. She'd become a total fan in twenty-four short hours. Seeing his hometown through Amy's eyes, he couldn't disagree. It was model-town America, a Main Street experience, filled with history, heart and hope. But not for them because there was no work here for him and far too many memories. He'd already seen how his sudden reappearance hurt Dave's son. Having Drew in town would poke salt into too many old wounds. "I'm glad you liked it, honey."

"Not liked. *Loved.*" She met him eye to eye,

leaving no doubt about her intentions. "I could live here in a heartbeat, Dad."

"Be kind of tricky with me in Jersey, wouldn't it?" He laughed and changed the subject by moving forward to accept food bags from Josie Gallagher's delivery van. "Amy, can you take this in for me?"

"Sure."

He knew their conversation wasn't over, but it was over for the moment. He, Daryl and Kimberly had to stake out plans during the afternoon and blend while doing it.

"I'll take the tray." Daryl smiled at Josie, and the way she met his smile said Josie made this delivery personally for a reason.

"Josie, can you stay?" Kimberly took the last bags from her cousin, but Josie shook her head.

"No, we're getting prep work done for the supper rush, but I wanted to make sure you guys were well taken care of. Let me know when you run the menu past the bride—"

"And her mother," Drew warned.

Josie laughed. "I've handled mothers before. Including my own. It's all good."

They took the food to the upstairs break room, and once they were done eating, Allison shooed them out the door. "Amy and I've got cleanup. You three, well four—" she smiled at Rocky "—have work to do."

"Yes, go," Rory urged them. "Emily and I want to introduce Amy to the area merchants we work with. That way if we send her on a gofer mission, she knows where to go and who to see."

"We're out." Drew held the door open. Kimberly stepped through, and that soft summer scent nudged him again. Pretty, like her. Vibrant, like her.

If she's a distraction, you should leave her behind. Lives are at stake.

He squared his shoulders because the internal scolding held merit. He and Daryl needed to be on top of their game, which meant no flirting. Or thinking about what might have been. Or could be.

She flashed him an over-the-shoulder look just then, one of those quick, sweet smiles that grabbed him heart and soul. He'd need God's help on this one, no doubt, because not only was his attention split, but he *liked* it being split, and that could spell trouble.

Daryl climbed into the front passenger seat of the SUV as Kimberly situated herself behind Drew. He pulled away from the curb and said, "Daryl's going to chart the course for us."

Eyes down, she waved his comment off. "I'm reconstructing the flowers. Shelby and I decided to change things up so the florist wouldn't realize it was the same bride. I'm meeting with them at four, so if you guys could drop me off a little farther up Center Street before then, that would be great."

"You talked with Shelby?"

"Yes."

"On an unsecured line?" Her gaze flew up to meet his in the rearview mirror.

"I never thought of that."

"We have to think of that," he replied, grim. "Nothing gets said or done without—"

"You knowing about it," she finished for him. "Which was me, telling you about it now, right? Only I never thought of a secure line, which is your fault because if you wanted me to have one, you should have provided it. I have to talk to the bride, Drew. It's like…a rule."

He met her gaze, growled, then spoke succinctly as Daryl handed her an untraceable phone. "Our bad, Kimberly. We should have realized you'd be working evenings and mornings when we're not around. Use this one. I'll grab another from the hotel room later."

"Thank you, Daryl."

She made a face at Drew, a face he probably wasn't supposed to see, but he'd glanced back again as Daryl turned around. "Daryl's right. I should have equipped you. I thought telling you would be enough, but I forgot you'd probably work on your own time, not just office hours. Sorry."

* * *

He did sound sorry, and she felt bad about that.

Being a cop's kid had taught her that top security meant silence and secrecy. She'd taken that mind-set to Nashville, but the double whammy of politics and country music's finest put this wedding in unusual and combined crosshairs. "I should have thought of it myself, too. And have you considered that Nashville insiders aren't great at maintaining silence? There are tons of name-droppers who love pretending they're invited to things, and maybe even a few on the guest list who would use this wedding invite to show they made the cut. That's a big variable right there, isn't it? Once the new date goes out?"

"We're including a vow of silence pledge that needs to be signed when they respond, but you're right. We don't have the wedding venue address on the invitations, though, and people will be picked up in limo buses and taken to the Abbey."

"And Miss Tara and I just listed a three-day marriage and spirituality retreat on the Abbey website to cover the wedding dates," Darryl explained. "We fed it to their Twitter feed and Facebook page. It's a full-capacity event, so they can't accept further registrations, a perfect subterfuge."

"You do web design?"

Daryl laughed. "In my spare time."

"The florist should deliver everything to a neutral but normal spot," Drew added.

"Thought of that," Kimberly replied, hoping to smooth over the unsecured phone call fiasco. "They're delivering to the East Seneca Inn and Conference Center at eleven a.m. Our team will then redeliver to the Abbey at noon."

"Is that enough time to get things done?"

Kimberly shrugged. "It's less time for someone to figure out what's going on and mess things up, so yes."

"Who's making the delivery?"

"We are. Me, Rory and Em. Nothing strange or unusual about bridal planners organizing flowers. We'll leave cell phones at home so they can't be tracked by GPS, and we're using an unmarked delivery van rented under an alias. Does Jo know to list the catering order as a retreat instead of a wedding on her books if we go with them for the food?"

"I did that," Daryl told her. "I stopped by earlier, pretending to want breakfast. Of course, I did have breakfast because I can't imagine walking away from that place without enjoying a meal."

Kimberly smiled because she was pretty sure

the food was only a portion of Daryl's attraction to the Bayou Barbecue.

"You're having fun with this, aren't you?" Drew raised a brow as he pulled off into a shaded parking area along a grove of trees. Daryl stepped out and shot a series of quick pictures, using about ten seconds, total, before he was back in the car, ready to move on.

"I've had to use alternative locations and timing in Music City," she reminded him. "Not to this extreme, but enough to ensure galas, openings and fan events are as safe as I can make them."

"You miss it?" Daryl wondered. He met her eyes in the mirror again. "The crazy fun of Nashville, the nice folks, Music Row?"

She had, at first. But now that this wedding had taken over her life, she'd barely thought about Nashville. That was an amazing thirty-six-hour turn-around. "I did. But the more time I'm here, and being kept busy—" she exchanged a smile with Daryl "—I don't. Something about being back home feels right."

"Even with your daddy bein' sick and all?" Daryl asked.

"Maybe more because of that," she told him. "Knowing Dad's in a fight for his life makes me more patient with little things."

"Like sisters?" Drew wondered. Amusement

softened his voice. Did that mean she was absolved for the phone mistake? She hoped so, or it could become a long afternoon.

"Like sisters and security men," she replied. When he smiled, she figured she'd been forgiven. "Drew, how are you handling the change of date with the musicians for the ceremony and the reception? Shelby's using some Nashville favorites and two Manhattan friends. Are they forewarned about the security and are they able to reschedule?"

"Three of them have committed to the new date. The Nashville crowd is tight." He pulled under a shade tree in the Abbey's parking lot and gave Rocky the go-ahead whistle. "I'm more worried about the two friends from the New York City than the country music crew. But they've been visited by security personnel, so they understand the importance of keeping this quiet."

"It can't be an easy way to live." She made the observation softly, not directing it toward either man, but both acknowledged her words.

"It's a practiced art," Daryl said. "Like anything else, you get used to it."

Kimberly was pretty sure she'd never get accustomed to living with the security threats. Drew added, "Shelby's doing this for her father, just like you are. Rick's got a shot at a dream, a big dream. Shelby's willing to let his dream rank first on the list. Like you did when you came back to Grace Haven."

"The out-of-work scenario made my decision easy," Kimberly told him, but Drew lifted his eyes to hers once he climbed out of the car.

"A lot of people would have made that a reason not to come home, Kimber. They'd have played the out-of-work, need-to-interview cards and settled for daily updates."

She couldn't imagine turning her back on her parents like that. "Not me.'

"Not everyone's got your philanthropic nature," he replied. Then he redirected his attention to the perimeter of the site. "Daryl, can you photo frame the exterior? We can map out security ports later. Kimberly and I will do the inside, and then we'll all meet with Tara to touch base on what's been decided."

"I've got it."

Daryl moved west as Kimberly and Drew crossed the broad walkway leading to the center chapel doors. "Security ports?"

"Strategic camera stations placed so that I have eyes and ears where they're least expected."

"You don't mean…"

"Yes, I do. Female and male agents stake everything."

"Nothing is safe." She scowled as she rang Tara's bell.

"On the contrary, it's ultrasafe, and, yes, we maintain a presence throughout. But not to spy on people. To ensure safety. And that's a big difference."

Drew understood the rigidity of security better than most, because he'd lived the downside. Judging by the look on his face, risk was something Drew Slade took very seriously.

Chapter Eight

"Good! You're here!" Tara swung the door wide a few moments later. "Daryl and I did the setup plan yesterday. He did a wonderful job of putting my parents' concerns to rest, and he did amazing things with our website that made it look like ours, but with an overthrow that kicks in when anyone looks at it. They see the coming month's schedule as being full of retreats and an updated news feed for the missions. I don't think anyone would have a thought of the wedding being here."

"That's the goal." They sat around the large office table and manually took notes about supplies, deliveries and timing. About an hour in, Tara sat back and stared at them.

"What's wrong?" Drew asked.

"You okay, Tara?" Kimberly reached out a hand to her cousin's arm. "You look pale."

"I should be pale," Tara insisted. "And so should you. We're planning every last detail of a very important wedding, with the possible, no—make that *probable* next president of our country, and you two are plowing through like it's nothing. But what if something goes wrong? What if we miss a beat? What if there's a terrorist threat that sneaks through despite your careful planning and watchful eyes planted all over the Abbey and the grounds?"

Drew didn't hesitate. "We shoot 'em."

Tara stopped talking, dumbstruck, but then she burst out laughing as if his solution was the most normal thing she'd heard all day. "Okay, then. Glad we've got that settled."

She looked down to reorganize categories on her paper, but Drew touched her arm. She looked up. Mixed emotions played across her face. "First we pray," he assured her. "Then we prepare. And then we pray again. Most likely nothing will happen. It doesn't usually, or you'd be hearing it on the news, wouldn't you?"

"Or they'd keep it a big, dark secret so we little folks wouldn't worry," Tara scolded.

Drew burst out laughing. "Put your conspiracy theories on hold, okay? We have to be prepared—that's the simple truth of the matter. Once we've prepped everything, we rarely have to use those preparations. But how bad would it be for us to enter into an event like this unrehearsed?"

"Awful."

He nodded. "Exactly. Can we see the kitchen setup, the coolers and freezers?"

"Of course." She walked them into the kitchen, and while Drew took photos and measurements, Tara tugged Kimberly aside. "This isn't making you crazy?"

It wasn't, and Kimberly was more surprised than she wanted to let on. "I thought it would, but no. In fact, it's nice to have Drew and Daryl around to take charge of the security aspects. I used to have to do a lot of that myself. This time, I'm just doing what I'm told."

Tara's eyes widened. "The Kimberly I know was never big on doing what she was told. Who are you, and what have you done with my cousin?"

Kimberly's laugh brought Drew's attention their way, so she lowered her voice but kept her gaze on him, just enough so he'd know they were talking about him. "Well. He's easy on the eyes."

Tara almost snort-laughed.

"And when he looks at me, it's like looking into the sea on a cloudy day, all grays, greens, bits of brown."

"A swoon-worthy description," Tara whispered.

It was, Kimberly realized. "Deservedly so."

If Drew suspected the subject of their conversation, he gave no indication as he completed his on-site inspection. When he and Daryl had finished up, he shook Tara's hand. "You're being a great sport about all this, Tara. We're grateful."

"My pleasure," she told him. He moved down the wide front steps at an easy pace, then paused and turned back. "And it's never a bad thing to be called swoon-worthy, I suppose."

Tara's eyes went wide. "How did—"

"You heard us?" Kimberly turned, met his grinning gaze and frowned. "How?"

"Secrets of the trade," he quipped. When he tried to move, Kimberly stopped him in his tracks.

"You carry an amplifier to hear conversations at a distance."

"Not always." His smile went broader. "But I thought today would be a good day to test it on-site."

"I—"

He stopped her tirade with one finger pressed against her mouth. "I had to test the system here to check for interference from kitchen equipment, sensors, Wi-Fi and so on. How did I know you'd be singing my praises? And think of it this way." He looped an arm around her shoulders and started back down the steps. "That was pretty nice stuff to hear."

"Maybe I knew you were wired," Kimberly shot back. "Maybe it was a setup, to see if you were listening."

He stopped their progress long enough to catch her gaze. Hold it. And, oh, the look in his eyes, the invitation to know him better. All there. For her. But there was too much in their pasts and a flood of uncertainty in their futures. If Kimberly had learned anything recently, it was that she craved certainty. Maybe that's why the thought of joining her friends in marriage had appealed so much. "Then I would say thank you for all the nice words," Drew told her. "Even if you didn't mean them. But..." He opened her door for her and waited as she climbed in, then closed the door. "I'm stoked because I'm pretty sure you did."

She had, so what was there to say? Daryl texted that he was near the base of the driveway. When they picked him up there, Kimberly looked at him and laughed. "Nice outfit."

"Thanks. If anyone asks, I'm ornithologist Byron Ross from USC doing some fieldwork on the nesting habits of migratory East Coast birds."

"What happens if a real birder stumbles into you while you're scoping things? Can you talk the talk?"

"I can," Daryl assured her. "Taking on a persona you can't back up can be a suicide mission in undercover work. My daddy loved birding and he took me by his side while I was growing up. It's come in useful a time or two."

"I'm sure it has. What's next on the agenda?"

"We make note of every garbage can, receptacle, niche, ledge or anything where someone can easily drop a backpack or duffel bag," Drew told her. "We number them, and each area becomes the responsibility of a team member when they arrive for the presweep in four weeks. But first, we drop you at the lower end of Center Street so you can walk to the florist and make arrangements."

"All right." She pulled an electronic notebook out of her purse.

"No electronic footprint, remember?" Drew frowned at her through the rearview mirror.

"It's a dummy account set up because we work with this florist all the time. If I walk in there with a composition book, she's going to know something's up. If I scroll notes into this with no names or dates, I can transfer them later and I don't raise her suspicions."

"Works for me," Daryl said. "I have to say it's a real pleasure working with someone who's got some experience in these things."

"Thank you, Daryl. It's nice to be appreciated

by at least some of my coworkers." She poked Drew in the back.

His laugh said he was unoffended.

"Being a cop's kid and working Music Row gave me an inkling of this. We've sent a lot of red herring cars in and out of concert venues to steer people off track. I'm actually having fun, although I probably shouldn't admit that."

"Tell me how much fun you're having the week of the event, when every trash can and barrel and flowerpot is scoured repeatedly. Or removed from the areas." Drew pulled over at the curb a few blocks away from the florist. "Got your cell on?"

"I do."

"Good. I'll see you tonight."

"Okay." She stepped onto the curb, slung her bag over her shoulder and shut the door. He didn't pause or wave or smile. Those actions might draw attention to them, and that was the last thing they wanted to do.

But the simple words *I'll see you tonight* filled her with anticipation.

She was silly. There was nothing between her and Drew. He was leaving as soon as this wedding was completed, and she'd be working in Grace Haven for as long as her parents needed her.

But for just a moment, when he'd tossed that

everyday phrase at her, she wondered what it would be like to come home to Drew and Amy every night. To laugh and tease and hang with Drew, a kid and a dog.

The all-American image warmed her, but she refocused her thoughts as she walked into the florist shop. The original order had been for colors of the season, total October.

Today's order was a complete about-face and for a different weekend. If Kimberly played her part well, she'd walk out of the shop in an hour and Priscilla Evans wouldn't be the wiser. She'd messed up by calling Shelby on her personal phone. She wanted the florist do-over to go off without a hitch.

You want Drew to be proud of you.

She did. The admission should have worried her, but the thought of seeing those camo eyes directed her way, smiling, made it all worthwhile.

Dog days of summer.

Hot and muggy had been the rule of the day late into the afternoon, so Drew brought Amy and Rocky down to the lakeshore for some cool respite.

An incoming text from Rick said he was available for a ten-minute conference call. Amy was delighting Rocky by launching a stick into the water repeatedly, and not minding when the dog gave himself a good shake-off as needed. Drew placed the call from his spot on the edge of a weathered picnic table about thirty feet away. "Rick, it's Drew. What's up?"

"I had a minute and wanted to check in," Rick answered. "I've read the reports you've sent me, but the sound of your voice is a better indicator of whether I should be concerned or breathe easy."

"Easy on all counts," Drew assured him. "Mostly because your daughter and the wedding coordinator are amazingly cooperative and not throwing land mines my way. If this status changes as the date draws close, I may rethink my position."

Rick laughed. "That's a relief. I know Shelby's putting up a good front here. She's being helpful and supportive, and, man, she's a vote getter. When she talks, the young voters listen. Of course, being engaged to Travis brings in a grassroots segment I might not have won over otherwise, so that's a bonus. Shelby seems okay with all the wedding prep. Linda is another story."

Drew and Linda Vandeveld got along well as long as he did everything Linda's way. This time, that wasn't about to happen.

"She told me you changed almost everything

they'd planned and that Shelby's going along because I'm working her too hard on the campaign trail and she just wants it over and done with."

"First, you should buy Linda flowers more often because she has to put up with you and me," Drew told him. "Second, she's right that we changed a lot of things because the family status is different than it was. Shelby understood that, and, according to the wedding planner, Shelby is the number one person we have to please. Third, we're running everything by Shelby so she's part of the decision-making process, but she's letting us have our way, mostly because she thinks your campaign is more important than a wedding."

"It's not, of course."

Drew cleared his throat. "When the guest list swells to repay political favors, it loses sheen from a bridal perspective."

"You think I'm exploiting the occasion."

"I think you're doing what's expected of the party candidate," Drew told him frankly. "That doesn't make it wrong."

"But it does make it expedient."

"Slightly self-serving."

"Is that supposed to make me feel better?"

"No. What should make you feel better is that Shelby's a great young woman and she doesn't mind because she sees your candidacy as the greater good."

"What did I do to deserve a kid like that?" Rick asked.

"You raised her to love God and her country. Not a bad combo."

"We can secure this setting?"

Drew nodded as a familiar shape moved across the nearby intersection, heading toward the lakefront park. The sight of Kimberly in shorts and a tank top made him have to work to keep his attention focused on Rick. "Yes. We'll let the feds worry about *you*. We'll cover the venue."

"Can we make it seem normal, Drew? Mostly?"

Rick sounded a little tired, or maybe just mad at himself for letting the campaign bump Shelby's wedding to a distant second place. "Yes. We're blessed to have a one-of-a-kind event planner in on this. Her background is in country music and police work, she's worked major events in Nashville and she's got the inside track on the country scene."

"I can't remember you ever using glowing terms like that in the past."

"Well, I've never done wedding security for you before."

Rick's grunt said he wasn't exactly buying Drew's explanation, but he let it go. "Keep me updated as needed. We're stumping at the big arena here tonight, but I wanted to touch base with you and make sure I wasn't overlooking anything with this wedding."

"We're good. I'll share concerns if there are any. You harvest votes."

"One last thing. Did I hear you and this event planner suggested barbecue for the reception?"

"We did."

"My wife is going to ream you. Travis is thrilled. Shelby thought it was a great idea, and all Linda could see was one of Travis's friends slurping barbecue sauce on someone's designer gown."

"We'll stock the restrooms with stain remover sticks."

Rick laughed and hung up as Kimberly reached Drew's side. The sight of her in everyday clothing took him back in time. Kimberly had always been the Energizer Bunny Gallagher, on the go, ready to jump into the game of the moment. A total tomboy.

She didn't look like a rough-and-tumble tomboy now, even in the casual attire. She looked... beautiful. A fact he needed to ignore no matter how hard it was. "How'd the florist appointment go?"

She bumped knuckles with him as she eased one hip onto the table. "Crushed it."

"And she or he wasn't suspicious?"

"No reason to be. We squeeze in last-minute

clients whenever possible, and with Dad's illness, people are cutting us slack. Besides, she was thrilled to get the price tag on this event, and she's calling a local farmer to secure the pumpkins and gourds we'll need to put together this new look. We've tossed the autumn bouquets in favor of gilded fall harvest and canning jar lanterns. Country shabby chic gone upscale."

"Gilded pumpkins sounds weird to me." Drew kept his eye on Amy and the dog, but he wasn't unaware of Kimberly's proximity. Cotton, fresh and clean, like newly folded laundry, spritzed with a hint of that fruity floral stuff. Oh, hc was aware, all right.

"Well, you're a man."

He turned then, grinning. "I was afraid you hadn't noticed."

Did the flush on her cheeks mean something? Or was it the August sun?

"Kimberly, watch me hit that buoy!" Using pinpoint accuracy, Amy hurled the stick and hit the marking floater as Rocky launched himself back into the water to swim for it.

"Awesome!" she called before shifting her attention back to Drew. "She's got quite an arm, Drew. Does she play baseball? Or softball?"

"Yes, but not this past summer. I wasn't there to run her back and forth like I usually do."

"She should be playing," Kimberly declared. "That's a God-given talent right there."

"It's hard when you're working an hour away," he admitted. "And that's if everything is smooth. On a bad commute night or if I'm in the Manhattan office, it's longer. When I was just working corporate, it worked out all right. But once we hit the campaign trail, everything got bumped."

She stared at him. "At that rate, you spend over five hundred hours a year commuting instead of hanging with the kid. I don't get it."

"Gainful employment. Life in the tristate area is unaffordable unless you're raking in monster bucks, and I wanted her in a good school district even if it meant a longer commute."

She directed her gaze toward Amy. "I'm sure she'd vote for more time with her dad. Her Team Slade mentality seems pretty ingrained."

"That's why kids don't get to make the decisions," he answered. "It's my job to think about finances, safety, education, neighborhood and opportunities."

"Do you think our parents stumbled into living here by accident?"

Her question threw him off track. He glanced around. "I don't know what you're talking about."

"Grace Haven is gorgeous now," she explained, "and it was a great little town back then, but do you think they knew how much better this was than so many other places?"

She was right. He'd had a dream childhood here; they all had. He'd shoved that realization aside at some point, letting the loss of his buddy overshadow years of good times. "Maybe it's not so rare as it seems," he offered softly. "Maybe you and I took a wrong turn after Dave died and forgot to weigh in all the good stuff."

Kimberly had come to the same conclusion. That's exactly what they'd done. Ironic that it took coming home for both of them to see it. "I wonder if she'd like to play on the fall league team."

"We'll be gone by the beginning of October," Drew argued.

"That gives her a month and a half," Kim answered. "She'll have to be in school here for September, right?"

"Yes." He sounded hesitant, as if he hadn't really faced his current lack of options.

"So?" Kimberly eased off the table and faced him. "Why not keep her busy with a chance on the team while she's here? She can run and throw. Is she any good with a bat?"

"Better than good. She's got quick wrists."

"Then give her the opportunity to shine. The kid's got talent, and Coach Cutler is a gender-neutral guy. If a girl can make his team, she plays."

He stared, surprised. "You mean play on the boys' team?"

"If she makes it, she plays. And Corinne says the coach is awesome. He's developed a lot of great young players."

"She'd play with Callan?"

"He's a little older, but again, it all depends on the skill level of the athlete. Come on—you know all this. You played here."

"This wasn't part of the plan," he argued, but she'd piqued his interest. "Amy was supposed to be safely tucked in a fun and challenging athletic camp, then a boarding school at least through January."

"Well, she thwarted that, didn't she?" Kimberly laughed up at him. "What were you going to do about school? Have her skip a month?"

"No, I just hadn't gotten that far ahead in my thinking," he admitted. "But you're right, I'll need to take care of things tomorrow. Get her registered. Which means having her pediatrician send her records to the school and get anything else they need. Kids complicate things." He said it with a pretend glare in Amy's direction, but Kimberly read the truth. He loved his daughter. Amy's age meant that she'd been born before Dave died, but there had never been any mention of Drew having a child, and folks knew these things in small towns.

Drew must have read her mind. "Her mother died just before Amy was three years old."

Kimberly winced. "I'm so sorry."

Drew's strained expression said he shared the emotion. "We met while she was in grad school at the University of Rochester. We had a lot of fun together back when I didn't weigh up consequences like I do now. We parted ways when she graduated. She wanted me to move downstate. I refused, not knowing she was pregnant. Then we lost Dave. I felt like a loser, like nothing I did was right, and Eve called me the next year to say we had a daughter."

"That's quite a year."

"It sure was. I think hearing about Amy saved my life." He watched as Amy dashed around the park trees with Rocky in pursuit. "I felt so guilty about Dave's death. I couldn't sleep. I couldn't eat. I couldn't function. I was a danger to myself and others on the force."

His admission showed her how foolish she'd been. She thought he'd dealt with Dave's death and moved on. While her family recognized the danger in police work, Kimberly had laid the blame squarely at this man's door because a good partner always had your back. He hadn't—

and Dave had died. Shamed by her own shallowness, she listened quietly, at last.

"When I learned about Amy, I resigned from the force and moved downstate."

"You started over."

"Not at first," he admitted. "I wasn't quite done being stupid. I drank too much and did a pretty good job of alienating most of Eve's family and friends. Eve's parents are affluent people who were probably appalled by my behavior, but through them I ran into Rick Vandeveld. He saw something redeemable in me."

"He gave you a job."

"Starting at the bottom in security, yes. He gave me a hand up at a time when I hated myself. He showed me how important it is to be a great dad, a hard worker and a man of faith. I owe him a great deal."

"When Amy's mother died..." Kimberly wasn't sure how to phrase her question with sensitivity. "Weren't her grandparents a factor in Amy's care?"

"You mean did they want to keep their only grandchild instead of letting her be raised by her rabble-rousing father?"

"It couldn't have been easy."

"It wasn't, but I was working for Rick then, and I'd stopped drinking. And Eve and I shared time with Amy. They didn't like it much, but

Eve understood me better than most. She knew having a child would breathe life back into me. And she was right."

"She sounds nice, Drew."

This time he turned to face her. "She was. We both realized we weren't meant to be together, and she was engaged when she was killed in an accident. And then Amy was with me."

"Well you've done a great job because she's a delightful kid."

"Thank you. I think so. Right now she's a great kid with a very wet dog."

Rocky loped their way, paused and shook, spraying droplets of lake water all over them. "Amy, you did that on purpose."

"I did no such thing." Her grin belied her words. "I just happened to come this way. Rocky did the rest. Can we take a walk along the lake?"

"You're not hungry?" Drew paused. "Are you feeling all right?"

"Fine. I'm never real hungry when it's hot like this."

"Me, either," Kimberly agreed. "Then fall hits and I want to eat every high-carb comfort food known to man."

"Right!" Amy smiled in instant agreement. "We're so weird."

"No argument there." Drew laughed as Amy poked his arm, then slung an arm around her shoulders. "Come with us, Kimber. It's a perfect night for a walk along West Lake Road."

Kimberly glanced at her watch.

"I'll make sure we're back in time for your mother's phone call," he promised. "And maybe we can grab a basket from the Shrimp Shack on our way back. We can munch and walk, a perfect summer supper."

She almost said no, but when he tipped his head slightly, their eyes met.

She blushed, inside and out, and then she had to say yes just to prove she was in complete control of this attraction. Whether she was or not didn't matter. She appeared to be in control, and that was enough for now.

"Will Rocky be all right with the neighborhood dogs?" Kimberly asked as they curved down the lakeshore street. "The folks on West Lake Road are fussy."

"They don't like dogs?" Amy asked.

"They don't like being disturbed is more like it, but I think if we're with the police chief's daughter, we're okay." Drew snapped Rocky's lead onto his collar. "And Rocky won't react to the other dogs unless I tell him to."

"I noticed that with Mags," Kimberly said. "He's trained to ignore other dogs?"

"Unless given a command, and then he does whatever needs to be done."

"Which wouldn't be pretty," Amy added. "I got a call from Grandma and Grandpa today."

"Reaming you for wasting their money by ditching camp?"

"No, Grandma said she understood totally and that the camp agreed to refund the money in return for them not suing because they had no idea I'd left. And Grandma said she was going to donate the money to a good cause, and I said it would be nice if she donated it to Rory's classroom of kids."

"Amy, that's so nice of you to think of that." Kimberly squeezed the girl's shoulder, impressed.

"Well, Rory had just finished telling me that some of the kids are from migrant families and might not have boots or warm coats to get through the winter, so it kind of made sense. Rory doesn't know yet," she added. "I thought it would be smart to wait until Grandma's check gets here."

"Kimberly? Out for a walk? And Andrew." Lieutenant Alejandro Gonzalez set aside his lawn clippers and walked toward them, smiling. "I heard you were back."

"News travels fast."

"I'm not so sure it was the news of being back or buying three tubs of buttered popcorn to support the baseball team. Bertie Engle was singing your praises when I passed by their place this morning."

The Engles were the best, supporting local groups long after they'd raised their own kids and could have shrugged things off. "They're good people."

"They are. Is this your daughter?"

"Amy, this is Lieutenant Gonzalez. He works with Kimberly's dad at the police department."

"Hi." Amy stretched out her hand quickly.

The lieutenant shook her hand and raised an eyebrow toward Drew. "Seems we've both done our homework."

Kimberly took that as her cue to walk on with Amy. "We're going to hook right at the next block and put in our shrimp order, okay?"

"Perfect." Drew's smile said she read the situation correctly. "I'll keep Rocky with me."

"Okay. Jandro, I'll call you later if there's any change with Dad."

"Thank you, Kimberly. And we'll keep praying."

Chapter Nine

Drew waited until Kimberly and Amy were out of earshot, put Rocky at ease, then faced the lieutenant. "I made sure I updated myself on command before coming into town."

"And when one of my officers spewed your name last night because you annoyed him, I figured I better find out why you were here."

"And?"

"I called Pete, he explained things to me and then I checked out your credentials. You've made quite a name for yourself in security, Drew."

Drew wasn't sure what he meant by that, because good security should be nameless and innocuous.

"It's not easy running security for big firms these days, and politicians are worse. So Pete and I were talking."

Drew waited quietly.

"He was wondering if you'd be interested in coming to work here. On the force."

"I would not." The words flew out before Drew had time to soften them. "I don't do police work. I do security. Big difference."

"A gun's a gun," Jandro argued sensibly. "And Pete told me your job description changes if Vandeveld gets elected. Why not resettle here if that happens? You grew up here, you know the geography, the townies, the layout by heart."

A frisson of unease met an ounce of new possibilities at the base of Drew's neck. "I'm not a cop anymore."

"You'll always be a cop," Jandro pointed out. "Not much sense pretending otherwise. I didn't mean to mess up your date," he went on, and motioned to wear Kimberly and Amy were disappearing around the corner. "But our department's looking at a series of unexpected changes. Pete thinks you'd fit in, and you have the experience to do a good job. I'd like you to at least think about it while you're in town. See if it's doable."

Ludicrous, yes. Doable? No. "Jandro, I—"

"Something to think about," the older man advised easily. "You've got two months before the wedding, plenty of time to give us a look-see and make a decision. Pete's run a clean department for almost twenty years. We need someone like that to take his place. Not just smart but wise. I think that person could be you."

Drew couldn't have heard him right. He glanced around, then met Jandro's eyes. "Are you talking about the chief's job? You're asking me to apply for the chief's job?"

"Yes, what did you think?"

Drew hadn't thought. He'd assumed they were talking about rejoining at the street-cop level.

"Just between you and me, if Pete beats this thing, he's going to retire. He and Kate want time to travel, do the things they've put on hold for thirty years. My wife's company is pulling her to State College, Pennsylvania, to head up the Eastern Region headquarters, so I'll be leaving in fourteen months. It would be wrong of me to apply for a job I know I'm qualified for but won't be here to do."

"That's an upright thing to do, sir."

"That's how we've always run things, and how we intend to see it stay," Jandro replied. "But that leaves us without a head man once Pete makes his announcement. There's no one in the department right now with the fairness and wisdom it takes to lead. We need a certain number of years and experience, Drew. You've got both." Jandro clapped a hand to his shoulder. "Something to think about. I told Pete I'd mention it if I saw you alone. And then you came walking down the street. But you head on now—I've kept you from two pretty girls long enough."

Drew started to walk on; then he swung back. "Lieutenant?"

"Yes?"

"Thank you."

The middle-aged man gave him a quick salute. "My pleasure."

His brain shuffled the information Jandro had shared as he approached the popular seafood dive on the elevated western shore. The opportunity the lieutenant offered was unexpected, but came at the opportune time. He'd already decided to set down roots with Amy.

Could it be here?

It was something to consider, but he needed singular focus right now. Jandro would need to be updated on the wedding time-change once the new details were confirmed. He crested the small hill and Kimberly waved him over to the far side of the casual eatery. The counter clerk handed them the broad, flat box filled with spiced fried shrimp, chicken and sweet potato fries, and Drew looked from Kimberly to Amy and back. "You decided you were hungry, I take it?"

"About the minute I smelled this stuff." Amy popped a hot chicken bite into her mouth, screeched and grabbed her water cup. "Oh, my gosh!"

"The sign says, Fresh, Hot Food." Drew pointed out the banner-sized signs hanging on all four half-open walls. "They mean it, kid."

"I'll say." She breathed deep to cool her mouth, then pointed outside. "Can we sit at one of the picnic tables and watch the boats go by?"

"Sure."

Kimberly led the way over, brushed crumbs from the table, then laughed at Amy's face. "Rustic is good, honey. And the sun is a natural disinfectant."

"You're sure it's okay?" Amy glanced around, unsure. "I could go get a cloth and wash this down."

"Oh, she's been in the city too long," Kimberly notcd. "The land of hand sanitizers on every corner has spoiled her for us common folk who dust off seats and tables the way normal folks do."

"Amy, it's fine. Most likely we won't die," Drew assured her.

"Hey, I'm just being careful." Amy frowned at both of them, then brushed crumbs off her bench seat. "Okay, I've got this. We brush old, germ-infected food off the table with our hands—"

"That way the birds get a snack later," Kimberly confirmed.

"And then we eat the food with those very

same hands." Amy sent a pointed smile their way. "Right now I wish I hadn't aced life science and didn't understand bacterial reproduction ratios."

Kimberly laughed harder. "You throw like a boy and talk like a scientist. You're a fun mix, kid."

Amy slid into her seat. "Thank you. In fairness to me, it should be stated that flocks of pigeons like to gather on picnic tables in our area, so rules may vary from state to state."

"I'll grant you that concession." Kimberly took one of the Cajun shrimp, popped it into her mouth and sighed once she swallowed it. "If I lived here, I'd eat here every night."

"Or at Josie's Bayou," Drew reminded her.

"Or Stan's," Amy added.

"I'm doomed." Kimberly made a face at them. "Too many good choices."

"Which means you don't cook?"

Kimberly made a face. "No. The cooking gene skipped me."

"Luckily, I do."

She paused. Caught his gaze. Stopped chewing. And when she tried to swallow, she started coughing, which wasn't the romantic gesture Drew was going for. He grabbed a glass of water and handed it to her. "You okay?"

"Almost."

"Dad watches the cooking channel."

"Amy." Drew put a warning note in his voice, one she was sure to ignore.

"Well, you do." She held up another chicken strip. "He makes me seasoned chicken when the weather's nice."

"Why when the weather's nice?" Kimberly asked. "You can't eat chicken in the winter?"

"I deep-fry out on our patio," Drew explained. "We're on the seventh floor, and I don't like to make the entire apartment smell like cooking oil, so…"

"But we've done a lot of takeout this year," Amy acknowledged. "Since the campaign got started, life's been different."

She wasn't complaining; she was stating a fact. So why did Drew suddenly feel like a first-class loscr for putting Rick's campaign ahead of time with his daughter?

"Life has a way of doing that to you," Kimberly agreed. "When you live in Grace Haven, you have nine months of perpetual motion. Autumn kind of roller coasts into Christmas and New Year's, but then it's as if the clock grinds down. Winter settles in and for three months everything goes slow and easy. Except for back-breaking shoveling, of course."

Drew grimaced on purpose.

Amy sighed. "I love snow, no matter what

Dad says. And I love being in a small town like this, even though it's not tiny, like I thought. It's just right."

"Drew! Hey, good to see you, how's everything?" A former high school teammate stopped by their table.

"Perry, it's good, man." Drew stood and shook his hand. "My daughter, Amy. And you know Kimberly Gallagher, don't you?"

"Only because I used to gaze from afar," Perry admitted with a smile. "Kim, I'm sorry about your Dad's health issues. He's on our prayer list at church. Tara filled us in, and she's keeping us updated."

"Thank you, Perry."

"You're welcome. Drew, where are you staying? Are you back for good?"

He shook his head, ignored Amy's pleading expression and motioned north as he shaded the timeline for security's sake. "We're using the rental apartment at the Gallagher house while we're in town. We'll head back downstate in November."

"Well, make sure you stop by the big Christkindl Market if you're still here, then. It's the first weekend of November."

"What's a Christkindl?" Amy asked.

"A German Christmas fair with all kinds of food."

"Lots of arts and crafts and unique things to buy," Kimberly added. "And a Christmas angel picked to wander the grounds and take pictures with kids."

"That sounds so beautiful." Amy sent a wistful look to her father. "A Christmas angel, Dad? How cool is that? Can we go? If we're here?"

"Aren't you supposed to be eating?"

Perry laughed as Amy scrunched her nose. "I'll let you guys get back to your food. I just wanted to say it's good to see you, man. Real good."

He clasped Drew's hand, and the solidity of the handshake and the words made Drew's world feel more balanced.

Kimberly's phone alarm buzzed. She stood, grabbed one last fried shrimp and held up the phone. "I've got to head back so I'm there when Mom calls. I'll see you guys in the morning."

He didn't want her to walk back home alone. He wanted to stroll with her, listening to the sounds of summer surrounding them, but it was time to clamp a firm lid on things even if he didn't want to. "See you then."

She headed down the short drive to the lower road along the shore. He tried not to watch, but he did watch, hoping she'd turn back and maybe smile his way. Wave.

She didn't, and that meant she understood the

self-imposed rules, but right now he'd like to kick the rules to the curb, put the past where it belonged and see what the future might hold.

They couldn't, of course. He'd follow her lead and tuck the attraction aside. "Kimberly is way fun."

So much for putting Kimberly on the back burner. "She's cool."

"And she wears the best clothes," Amy continued. "She always looks perfect, no matter what she's wearing."

He paused midchew and looked at her. "Since when did you start caring about clothes?"

Her answering frown and flush made prickles of unease race up his back.

"I don't really care about clothes," she assured him, but the way she said it meant the opposite was true. "I just think she looks great."

No argument there, and how was he supposed to stop thinking about Kimberly if his own daughter kept bringing her up? "She's beautiful, but did you know she was a tomboy just like you growing up?"

"No." Surprise and doubt lifted her brows. "I don't believe it, either. There are pictures all around her mother's office, of Kimberly, Emily and Rory, all in dresses."

"That's for effect," Drew explained. "Kate would want the office filled with feminine things because it sets the mood for formal events. But I don't think I saw Kimber in a dress until she was a high school senior, and that was by accident."

"How?"

"They'd rented a limo for the senior ball, the limo was in an accident and all the kids were stranded in the pouring rain. Kimberly's brother, Dave, and I heard the call, and we took our cars to the scene and gave the kids rides to the ball so they wouldn't be soaked to the skin. The other three girls were in tears."

"But not Kimberly?"

"No." Funny, he'd forgotten how nicely she'd taken charge with the other girls. They'd stopped back at the Gallagher house and Kimberly had taken the girls inside. A little fresh makeup, a blow-dryer and a spritz of hairspray later, they looked wonderful. "Kimberly doesn't panic. That's another thing you two have in common. So it's okay to be a tomboy, kid. And to clean up well."

She blushed, and that sounded the second nail in his father-of-a-preteen coffin. Liking clothes…blushing…

The reality of handling an adolescent and puberty by himself smacked him upside the head. With no babysitter, and an hour-long commute, there was too much unsupervised time in Amy's future.

But that was the future. This was now.

First thing tomorrow he'd set up the basement office to facilitate what he and Daryl needed to do as prep work for the wedding. And once Amy was back midday, he'd take her over to Grace Haven Elementary and get her registered.

And if she wanted to play ball for the next six weeks?

He'd give her the chance to try out. Kimberly was right. A talented athlete like Amy needed to pursue her own dreams. He'd forgotten that in the quest to help Rick attain his new goal, but being here in his old hometown made him remember that being a parent should come first.

He dropped some folded cash into a prayer box outside one of the gracious stone churches dotting Center Street as they walked back to the village.

"What's that for?" Amy asked, curious.

"I slip money into the first missions' box I see whenever God gives me a wake-up call. It's a way of saying thank you for trying to make a stubborn guy like me smarter."

"And you *just* had this wake-up call?" She gave him her famous "I know my Dad's crazy when—" look, brows up, skepticism marking her gaze.

"I did. How would you like to go with me tomorrow afternoon to get you registered for school? And then to see about trying out for the fall league baseball team?"

Her eyes went wide. Happy anticipation brightened her expression. Was he offering her false hope? He didn't mean to, but they needed to take care of these things, and if they both fell in love with this beautiful Finger Lakes town, that wouldn't necessarily be a bad thing.

He knew God could shut doors and open windows. He just wanted to be smart enough to know when he should stop knocking and start climbing through. He was approaching a fork in the road. And even with wedding security taking precedence, he needed to assess the coming months, their future.

Chiming bells announced the sunset, an old tradition among the Center Street churches. First one, then the other, ending with the melodic sounds of a hymn from the gracious stone church in front of them.

Amy gripped his hand tighter. "That is so beautiful, Dad. I love hearing that."

The bells fell silent as they crossed The Square.

"I'm sorry if I love it here too much."

Drew's heart sighed. His precious daughter felt guilty for wanting a normal life. He bent to meet her eye. "I love it here, too. I'd forgotten how much."

Her face softened, and she hugged him tight. "I really don't care where we live, Dad. As long as we're together."

The lieutenant's words came back to him. Had God put him here purposely, at a time when the town might need him as much as he needed to come home?

"You want ice cream?"

She laughed. "Always."

"Every August night deserves ice cream," he told her, and he hooked a right-hand turn back toward Stan's.

Amy's words touched his heart. She loved the town, yes. She'd made that clear.

But her earnest statement said she loved him more, and that made the option more special. He wanted change. They needed a home, a real home, and that's exactly what he intended to find once the election was over.

Could that long-awaited home be here, in Grace Haven?

Chapter Ten

"Mom sounded good, didn't she?"

Relief lightened Emily's tone. If spinning their father's prognosis to protect Emily and Rory was Kate Gallagher's goal, she'd done a good job of it tonight.

"She did." Rory faced her sisters with a more cautious note. "But I worry more when she sounds that confident."

"Why?" Emily asked. "Haven't the past few weeks been troubling enough? I'm going to grab her good news about Dad's treatment and run with it. We could all use a little pick-me-up right now."

"What do you think, Kimber?"

Kimberly had hoped they wouldn't ask the question directly. As much as she loved her mother, she couldn't lie to her sisters. "I think Mom needs us to be positive, so she paints a positive picture."

Rory accepted her words without challenge.

Emily frowned. "You think she's lying to us?"

Kimberly shook her head. "Not lying. You know Mom, Emily. She's great at handling the truth herself, but she likes to protect us."

"Not about this, surely." Emily stared at her, and as realization dawned, she took a step back. "She doesn't try to protect you, though, does she? She'll paint a rosy picture for me and Rory, but I can tell from your face that she's been up front with you, Kimberly. So maybe you should fill us in on what's really going on? Or have you been sworn to secrecy?"

"Emily, be fair," Rory cautioned. "Maybe Mom needs someone to talk to on the level, and if Kimberly is that person, isn't that a good thing?"

"Not if it means she thinks we can't handle the truth," Emily shot back. "For once I'd like to be considered mature enough to not only handle the truth but have my mother treat me like an adult."

"You're right, Em."

Emily stared at Kimberly, assessing.

"Can we sit? I've been on my feet most of the day, and I sure could use a chair right about now."

"The living room," Rory decided. "Way more comfortable."

They fell into cushioned seats around the great room, and Kimberly prayed she was doing the right thing. "Mom's been shading the truth to both of you. I told her she shouldn't. She didn't listen. She said if we stayed positive, it was easier for her to stay upbeat for Dad, so she's been feeding you false hope."

"Lying to us."

Kimberly shook her head. "No, but not telling you the whole truth, either. And she didn't want the worst-case scenario to leak back to the station house, so she tried to buy time."

"Are we going to lose Dad?" Rory asked the question straight-out, a question that had multiple answers.

"We might. Or the treatment might damage parts of his brain that leave him unable to function in some ways, and there's no way of knowing how destructive that might be. Only time and physical therapy can tell. Or it could be a total success. But the chances of a total success are less than forty percent."

Emily's skin paled. "But they've had good outcomes with this new treatment, even though it's experimental."

"Yes. But there have been very few people in the program because it's crazy expensive and not covered by insurance."

"Which is why Mom wanted to make sure we were available to run things this fall," Rory added softly. "The money from these events will pay for Dad's treatment."

"Right. It not only keeps business going—it could keep Dad alive." Kimberly shifted her attention to Emily. "I'm not saying what she's doing is right, Em. But she's not doing it because of you, or because she thinks you guys can't handle the truth. I think she's doing it for self-preservation, so she wouldn't be worrying about us while she was trying to be strong for Dad. Mom's strong, but she's too protective of us."

"And that got worse when we lost Dave."

Kimberly nodded. "Mom likes to run a smooth ship."

"And she's got great faith," Rory added, "but like most strong people, letting go and letting God take the wheel doesn't come easy for her."

"She's got faith in God but not faith in us," Emily stressed. "And that makes me feel like she doesn't think I'm strong enough to take over, to step in or even be trusted with the truth. How would you feel if she treated you that way, Kimberly?"

"Just like you're feeling," Kimberly admitted. "But we're at a crossroads right now. Rory thinks God put us here. I don't know if that's true, but I know we've got a chance to make choices and do this right for Mom and Dad. If we start with the three of us, being more understanding of each other, I think we stand a better chance of succeeding while Mom and Dad face this fight. The best way to show Mom and Dad the women we've become is to work together during trouble."

"Starting now," Rory said. She reached out and grasped each sister's hand. "And we start like Mom would, with a prayer."

"You're bossy for being the youngest," Emily mock scolded, but she squeezed each sister's hand lightly. "I'm in. On the prayer and the better attitude. I promise."

"Me, too." Kimberly returned the gentle squeeze. "Go for it, Rory."

"Lord, we thank You for this sisterhood. We ask You to bless us with warmth, grace, humor and faith as we help our parents through this difficult time. And, Lord, we ask You to heal our father, to give him more time here on earth and bless him with abundant health for years to come. Amen."

"Amen." Emily and Kimberly spoke together before Emily asked, "So. Do we let Mom know we're aware?"

"Yes." Kimberly answered quickly. "I think she'll actually be pleased to know we're all on the same page. But let's keep Dad's medical issues private. The police force already knows this is serious. They know Dad might not be coming back to his job."

"Which is why that vulture Brian keeps stopping by here and there," Emily added. "If Dad vacates his office, I think Brian is hoping for a special election and plans to run."

"Wouldn't the mayor appoint an interim to fill in for the next two years?" Kimberly asked. "That's how it's supposed to happen."

"You and I know that, but Brian's got it in his head to petition for a special election with his name on the ballot."

"How do you know this?"

"Bertie Engle told me he's been nosing around the sports boosters and the baseball organizations, looking for support."

"I heard the same thing at Callan's game last night," Kimberly admitted.

"Not for nothing, but we can't control any of that," Rory advised. Both sisters shifted their attention to her. "Whatever happens with the police force and Dad's job is in God's hands right now. I say we focus on what we can affect—Kate & Company and our lives here. If we do our best at that, the ripple effect will bring its own rewards."

"Young and sensible," Emily remarked, smiling.

"The Serenity Prayer." Kim indicated the framed print on the living room wall. "We change what we can."

"And leave the rest to God," Rory declared.

Kimberly longed to do that. When had she stopped? When they lost Dave or before?

Before, she realized.

She'd gone off on her own, had done well. And even in the heart of Music City, surrounded by faith-filled music and churches, she'd shrugged off the faith she'd known as a child. That made it easier to hate God when Dave was killed.

Change what you can.

Accept what you cannot change.

Be smart enough to know the difference.

The simple prayer had been Kate's mainstay for decades. Maybe it was time her oldest daughter took the gentle words to heart.

Time to think, to pray, to relax...

Drew wasn't sure if he should celebrate this new normal or go stark raving mad because for the past eight years, time had been a nonexistent commodity. Here in Grace Haven, with the wedding plans set to go, he had a chance to kick back.

He liked it.

Thanks to Kimberly's expertise, wedding plans were done. With the Secret Service in charge of Rick's safety, he wasn't needed on the campaign trail. Daryl would return to Manhattan over Labor Day weekend to make sure corporate security was running smoothly, and Drew was right where Rick wanted him to be for the coming weeks. But no one warned him that he'd fall in love with his hometown all over again.

His phone buzzed. The baseball coach's name appeared in the display. "Coach, hello. What's up?"

"I'm giving Amy a spot on the team," the coach told him. He hesitated, then went on. "Here's the problem, though. I know she might not be around next season, and it's likely to put some noses out of joint when I give her a position. Fact is, she's that good and I want the chance to help her polish a few moves before you guys leave."

The coach's decision to play Amy said a lot about his character. "Thanks, Coach. You're sure you're okay with this?"

"My team, my decision," the coach replied. "I'm not telling you this to worry you. I'll smooth it over. But if folks give you grief, that's why."

"You think they will?"

"A couple, yes. Some parents exaggerate their kids' skills. Some think their kid's guaranteed a spot, but baseball's a hustle game. I like hustle, and your kid's got it. I'll see you on the field at six tonight."

He called Corinne's number, but the call went straight to voice mail. She'd said she worked the overnight shift at the hospital, which meant she might be sleeping now.

How would Callan react to Amy being on the team? To Drew being there, night after night? The league games started Wednesday, the first day of school. Would bumping other kids off the team make Amy's opening days of school tougher?

He glanced at his watch, weighing the time. Amy needed school clothes. She had outgrown all her old things, and the uniform he'd thought she would be wearing at boarding school was no longer an option.

They'd need to go shopping. If there was one thing he hated, it was shopping for clothing. Single dads didn't have much choice.

Unless…

He moved to the main level of Kate & Company, saw Kimberly coming through the front door and pretended he was unaffected.

Allison smirked.

He ignored her.

Mags flew across the floor, her tiny feet tapping a quick rhythm on the hardwood and then were silenced by the thick deep-pile carpet.

"Hey, dust mop." Kimberly reached down to pet the pooch, then looked up at him. "Did you hear from Shelby's mother yet?"

"Approving the food? No."

Kimberly made a face. "If she's really opposed to it, we can change things up. I think the majority of the guests will love it, but maybe you were right. Not everyone sees good barbecue as wedding-friendly."

"Want me to feel her out? Call her?"

Kimberly shook her head as she started up the stairs. "I'll do it. I know they're crazy busy with the campaign, and she's got Shelby's two brothers on the trail with them. That can't be easy, trying to tutor them and meet all the commitments of a campaign."

"You're a nice person, Kimberly Gallagher."

She flashed him an over-the-shoulder smile as he followed her up the stairs. "I'm trying. I think I'm actually getting good at it."

"Practice makes perfect."

"That's what they say." She reached out to brush a fleck of something off his collar. The tips of very pretty fingers grazed his neck. The summer scent tempted him forward; therefore, he took a short step back.

"Amy made the baseball team. She's playing fall ball." He frowned, wishing something so simple didn't have complicated dynamics.

"And that's bad because?"

"Will Callan be able to handle having me around every night?"

Compassion softened her gaze as she listened.

"I get that they're both good ball players, but maybe I'm shoving in where I don't belong."

"Callan needs to move beyond his anger. Kind of like me."

Drew winced. "He's a kid without a father."

"It's better for him to face this now, don't you think? Rather than carry all this angst around through high school and college?"

"Maybe." He drew out the word slowly. "But I don't relish my role in all this. Even though it's deserved."

"It's not about guilt or blame, Drew."

When it came to Dave's kid, he wasn't so sure of that. Callan's anger showed him atonement might be long overdue, but inserting himself and Amy into Callan's domain seemed as if it might be more hurtful than healing, and how could he justify that?

Truthfully, he couldn't.

Drew was beating himself up.

She read it in the stern gaze, the rigid jaw. She'd been wrong to think he'd casually moved on with his life after Dave's death. The man before her had suffered, like her. Initially he'd seemed more at peace with the past, at least until he faced Dave's son.

"I'm glad the coach is giving Amy a chance. That's pretty cool."

"Me, too," Drew admitted. "She's happiest with a glove on one hand and a ball in the other."

"A chip off the old block, just like Callan."

A tiny muscle in his cheek jumped. "I hope it goes well. And that she loves being on the team. I can't wait to see her face when I tell her."

"But..." She studied him. "There's something else on your mind, isn't there?"

He exaggerated a look of pain to make her smile. It worked. "I've got a bad case of shop-o-phobia. School starts in a few days, and all we've got here is a knapsack and duffel full of camp clothes. Amy would have worn uniforms at Redfern. If she's playing baseball every night, and we're working during the day, when do I fit shopping in?"

She withdrew her phone, tapped her electronic calendar and held it up. "How about Monday afternoon? We can duck out at noon and be back by six. She's got everything she needs to play ball?"

"With her camp gear, yes."

She finished the notation in her phone and moved toward him. "Done, and I hope you don't mind me tagging along. I think it will go quicker that way."

"Mind? No, I don't mind. Not in the least, Kimber. Thank you."

He took her hand, sweet and polite, his tone laced with simple gratitude, and then…

Oh, then...

His gaze went tighter, wondering, as his eyes met hers. His eyes strayed to her mouth, but he didn't pause to ask permission.

She didn't want him to. The Drew she remembered, the guy she'd been attracted to for years, made decisions and stuck by them, and that's just what he did now as he lowered his mouth to hers.

Was it as wonderful as the teenage Kimberly imagined?

Better.

Unbelievably better.

And when he finally broke the kiss and pulled her into a long, warm hug, the rich, smooth beat of his heart felt as if she'd finally come home.

"I won't apologize." His voice sounded gruff and endearing, rolled into one deep, dear tone.

"I'd smack you if you did."

She felt his face move as he smiled. "And I'm not saying it won't happen again, Kimber."

She tried to pull back, but he kept her right there in his arms, against his heart. "Except—"

"Nope." He released her then and took a step back as he heard Amy and Rory approaching. "Remember the rules. I get final say in everything."

"Those rules referenced Shelby's wedding," she scolded.

"I've upgraded them to an all-inclusive mandate. Hey, kid." He stepped back to make more room for Amy. "Coach called, and you're on the team. Are you ready to head home, get changed and hit the practice field tonight?"

"Yes!" Delight spiked Amy's tone. "I can't believe I'm getting the chance to play on the same fields you did. Do you have any idea how cool this is?"

"Let's see how cool you think it is after tonight," Drew warned her. "Coach is a great guy, but I watched him last week. He's tough."

"Well, I'm a Slade," Amy told him, as if that said it all. "So no worries."

They turned to go, but before Drew followed her out the door, he gave Kimberly's hand one last squeeze, just enough to say he hadn't forgotten the beauty of their kiss.

Neither had she.

Chapter Eleven

"All right, Slade. Let's see what you've got." Coach Cutler motioned Amy over, waved Drew off and tossed Amy a jersey to use for the scrimmage. "You think you can handle second base?"

"Yes, sir."

"We'll give it a look." He jerked his head toward the field, and Amy trotted out to the center of the infield, looking confident.

"You scared?" Kimberly whispered as she came up behind him and poked him in the back.

"I'm currently fighting the urge to either throw up or go out there and help her."

Kimberly laughed softly. "That's good parenting, then. Let 'em fall, let 'em fail. It builds character."

"I heard your parents say that all the time." He dropped his gaze to hers, let it linger long enough to see color rise to her cheeks, then smiled. "They did well."

The scrimmage started. They found seats just below Corinne and Tee. When the first batter grounded out to second, Amy scooped the ball and sent a bullet to first base. When the batter was called out by a step, she gave a casual nod, made the "one out" sign with her pointer finger and reassumed her position.

Drew breathed.

His girl knew the game, just like he did. She was a Yankees fan, she had pinstriped pillows on her bed and her favorite gifts were tickets to Yankee Stadium.

"Smooth moves," Corinne said above him. "Watching those two out there takes me back twenty years or so, Drew."

He was just about to reply when the next batter hit a line drive toward Callan at shortstop. He fielded the ball cleanly, threw to first, then plowed into Amy as she was moving behind him for backup.

Amy hit the dirt hard.

Callan didn't stop to offer a hand up or apologize. He moved back to his position, held up the hand signal for two outs and pretended as if nothing had happened.

Drew had to hold himself in his seat. Amy had played in tough leagues from the beginning. She'd taken her share of hits, but not from her own teammates. At least not intentionally, and Drew had seen the whole thing. Callan had mowed her over on purpose, showing disrespect. Was it because she was a girl or his daughter?

Drew didn't know, but Callan outweighed Amy by an easy twenty pounds, and there was no room for bullying tactics in baseball.

"I'll kill him later," Corinne promised. Her firm tone said she was only half kidding. "He knows better, Drew."

Drew stayed quiet, watching, and when their team hustled in after the third out, Coach Cutler pulled Callan aside. His face and hand motions said Callan was getting the dressing-down he deserved. The boy's face darkened, and then he broke all the rules of baseball deportment by throwing down his glove and cap before he stomped off the field and toward the parking lot.

Corinne stood up, and Drew fully expected her to dash down the bleacher steps and race to the car to comfort her son.

She surprised him by yelling, "Batter up!" and then reclaimed her seat.

Drew turned. "You're not going after him?"

"And reward his bratty behavior? No, sir." She shook her head and handed him a bin of pretzels. "I came to watch a ball game, and that's what I intend to do. He can stew in the car all he wants, but it's way more fun being in the field or up at the plate."

"He'll be in big trouble when he gets home," Tee predicted.

"Hush, you. I'll handle your brother. You have your own host of interesting behaviors to contend with, I believe."

Tee grinned, and when she did, it was her father's smile and easygoing attitude that shone through. "Grandma says I'm a piece of cake compared to Callan. Of course, she also says Callan reminds her of Aunt Kimberly sometimes. Is that true, Aunt Kim? Did you have a temper like Callan?" She leaned down around Kimberly's shoulder, making it impossible to ignore the question.

"There might be a slight family resemblance." Kimberly reached up and tugged Tee's short hair. "Luckily we mature. Eventually."

"I can hardly wait," Corinne added. "But if he follows his aunt's footsteps, I've got a long road ahead of me."

"Worth it, though." Drew kept his gaze forward but nudged Kimberly's shoulder to let her know she was most definitely worth it. "Your cop buddy's here again."

"I see him. Working the crowd, a born politician."

As he watched Brian circulate among the

folks watching the scrimmage from the sides of the baseball diamond, Jandro's invitation came back to him. Two men he respected thought he could do the job. So did he, and the timing was perfect. Amy glanced his way as she hustled off the field at the end of the next inning. Her beaming smile convinced him.

He might not get chosen to fill Pete's shoes for the remaining years of his term, but he'd lose nothing by putting his name in for consideration.

"How come you didn't bring Rocky?" Tee wondered. "Everybody thinks he's a cool dog."

"He is," Drew agreed. "But when he's out in a crowd, he's working."

Tee frowned.

"He's a police dog," Drew explained.

"Right, a K-9 partner."

Duh, Slade. The kid's from a cop family. She knows the drill. "He can't turn it on and off automatically. So if he needs downtime, I leave him home."

"And when Rocky stares out the window, Mags goes ballistic, jumping up and down, barking like crazy." Kimberly held up her cell phone. A picture of Mags showed her paused, midleap, a flustered bundle of fur.

Drew winced. "I didn't know that. Sorry."

"We have video proof." Kimberly touched the screen. Their section of the bleachers heard the

Yorkie's protective yapping, and then Emily had zeroed in on Rocky's classic stoic countenance in the upstairs window. Cool, calm, unflappable, much like his owner.

"He totally ignores her." Tee laughed out loud. "And drives her crazy by doing it."

"It's a man thing," Kimberly assured her. She didn't look at Drew, but it felt like she had. "Although every now and again, it's good to let down your guard."

He'd let his guard down today, kissing her. And thinking of that kiss made him wonder when they might be able to try a repeat performance, which was exactly why he shouldn't be thinking of it.

A text from Daryl pushed his thoughts aside. Trouble.

He stood, palmed Tee's head with a smile and moved to the aisle. "Duty calls. Kimberly, can you get the kid home for me?"

"Glad to. Everything okay?"

"Daryl needs to go over a couple of things." He moved down the stairs and waved to Amy. When she nodded, he knew she understood.

He started his car, pretended not to notice Callan's glare from two cars down and headed south when he hit East Lake Road. Below the Abbey, where the tapering lake brought roads together,

Daryl waited in a graveled pull-off near a state-operated boat launch.

"What have we got?"

Daryl pointed up. A majestic view of the Abbey rose above them, the broad yard tapering to the tree line below. "Narrow water means someone could take target practice on the motorcade or guests. But how do you close down East Lake Road on an autumn weekend when we're already closing down West Lake Road and blocking boat traffic? This whole town's gonna hate us. And they're going to hate Rick."

Small businesses depended on summer and fall season weekends to make their living. The people living along the upper and lower lake roads might like to get out of their homes at some point. "And it's peak season for fall tourists, even without a festival that weekend.

"Temporary shutdown as people gather?" Daryl wondered. "A two-hour window?"

"Not enough," Drew replied. "We're going to make some people mad, Daryl. The downside of high security in modern times."

"Let's plug it into the computer model tomorrow," Daryl suggested. "Didn't Kimberly say they were picking up the flowers on this side of the lake and transporting them in?"

"Yes."

"Well, that can't happen," Daryl offered mildly.

"We need everything in place forty-eight hours prior so we have full security shut down."

"Agreed. And we need to see the reverend tomorrow. I want all principal players sheltered in place on Friday. We'll give them the full wing of the retreat center so none of the family or attendants are on the buses."

"But we deck out two of the transport buses to look wedding-friendly."

"Yes."

"You gonna tell Kimberly?"

"No."

"She's not going to like that."

"She'll understand after the fact."

Daryl's wince said he wasn't so sure. Neither was Drew, but security ranked first on the priority list. Kimberly was great at her job, but the size of the Gallagher family alone meant one wrong word could leak information. Nothing was going to go wrong with this wedding, and not just because it was a presidential candidate's daughter getting married.

It was his friend's kid, and Drew would do whatever he needed to make sure Shelby had a beautiful day. The only way he could keep Kimberly in the dark was to back away from his growing attraction to her. After sharing that downright amazing kiss, the thought of pushing Kimberly away made September seem ridiculously long.

"Thanks for bringing her home." Drew slung an arm around Amy's shoulders and tweaked her ball cap once Kimberly parked the car that evening. "How'd the scrimmage go?"

"Two walks and two pop-ups." Amy's disgusted tone said she was mad at herself for not hitting well. "We're playing this team again tomorrow night, then practicing three days in a row."

"You'll find your sweet spot," Drew told her. "New place, new pitching."

She yawned. "I'm grabbing a shower and going to bed."

"No ice cream?"

"Too tired."

"You did okay tonight, kid." Kimberly fist-bumped Amy. "It was pure Slade, through and through."

"Can we go to the batting cages tomorrow?" Amy asked as she reached for the screen door handle.

"No time. Sorry."

"Okay." She went inside, lugging her equipment bag over her shoulder.

"She's pretending not to be disappointed."

"Welcome to the life of the single parent."

Drew shrugged one shoulder. "If it doesn't work on my schedule, it doesn't happen. Unless her grandparents are in town."

"What if I take her?" Kimberly suggested. "Maybe a few rounds with the pitching machine will boost her confidence."

His expression shifted slightly; then he shook his head. "Amy knows she wasn't supposed to be here in the first place. She made choices that put her in this position. She knows I have to work, that I'm not at her beck and call, and that's the consequences of changing the game."

"Oh." It took every bit of Gallagher gumption for Kimberly to shut her mouth and not say more. "Okay, then."

She started up the rock path her parents had created two decades before, waiting for him to call her back.

He didn't.

That stung.

She'd spent the day thinking about Drew and that kiss, the sweetness of old and new feelings converging to make a fresh beginning.

His cool brush-off brought that all to a dead stop.

She walked into the house, determined. She'd been tossed aside by her former fiancé. She'd been dismissed by the company she'd served for seven years. She wasn't in the mood to be shrugged off again by anyone. From this point forward, she'd work with Drew as needed, and nothing more than that, because no one would be allowed to treat Kimberly Gallagher casually ever again.

She thought the public humiliation of being dumped personally and professionally had smartened her up. Not enough, it seemed, or Drew wouldn't have claimed that kiss.

She didn't stop to chat with Rory as she cruised through the living room and climbed the stairs. She went to bed scowling and woke up pretty much the same way, and that wasn't Drew's fault. It was hers. But she'd make sure she wouldn't be tempted again. And if she was tempted?

She'd shrug it off as bad news, all around.

Chapter Twelve

Kimberly was managing to avoid him despite their working arrangements, and Drew wouldn't have thought that possible.

Wrong.

If he was in the office, she was out of office.

If he was at home, her parking spot next to the family garage stayed empty.

When he and Amy walked the neighborhoods and visited the school, Kimberly was nowhere to be found.

You miss her.

He shrugged that off as ridiculous, but when she texted him a message saying she couldn't go shopping with them on Labor Day, as she'd promised, he went upstairs to have a face-to-face discussion.

"Do you know where she is?" He might have

growled the words at Allison, or maybe it just felt as if he was growling.

"Of course. She's planning a holiday wedding at the Evergreen mansion. They're doing a walk-through and tasting."

"Was this scheduled in advance?"

Allison shook her head. "Just in yesterday. The bride was at a wedding we did at MacCauley's Vineyards and we impressed her, so Kimberly jumped right on it, understandably."

"Understandably?" He lifted one brow in question.

"We just paid out twenty thousand for Pete's initial treatments." Allison kept her voice soft. "An average wedding nets about five thousand profit, so if we're going to keep up payroll, utilities and benefits, grabbing work when it's available is huge. And winter is quiet."

He knew that, and the dollar and cents of Pete's treatment humbled him. He was focused on one wedding. Kimberly was overseeing at least a dozen separate events, knowing each success allowed her father and mother necessary time and medical treatment.

He called Jandro Gonzalez from his cell phone. "Lieutenant, can I meet with you tomorrow to go over some things concerning the Vandeveld wedding?"

"Glad to. Is ten a.m. good for you?"

"Perfect. I'll be there."

He arrived at the station house the same time Kimberly walked across The Square the next morning, her messenger bag slung across one shoulder. "I'm not late, am I?"

"For?" Drew asked.

"Our meeting with Jandro. He called me to say he was running a few minutes late," she explained lightly, as if it was all right that he'd left her out of the loop, but her cool-eyed gaze said otherwise. "But here he is now, so we're all set."

They weren't all set, and she was about to find out he'd made changes without consulting her. They gathered in Jandro's office, with the door closed, and Drew explained the gravity behind the double road closings and keeping Travis's and Shelby's families sheltered in place prior to the wedding.

He finished, and if looks could kill, the expression on Kimberly's face said he was a dead man. "You can't be serious." She stared him down, glanced at Jandro, then back at Drew. "We'll be hated, and Kate & Company can't afford to be hated. We've got bills to pay, and if people get mad at us for totally disrupting their September business earnings, it's not you or the

Vandevelds they'll get even with. It's us, and that's not fair."

"Can we afford to have the family susceptible?"

"No, of course not, but there's got to be a better way," Kimberly argued. "What if there's an emergency? How do first responders get through?"

"They'd be allowed through, of course," Drew replied. "But casual travel would be completely curtailed, including air, land and water."

"No boaters?"

Jandro's expression said he wasn't all that happy, either. "Do we have any known threats against the senator, the bride, the groom or any of the guests?"

Drew slid a sheet of paper across the table. "These are the current threats involving candidates and their families. As you can see, while most are probably pranks, we have three which are labeled credible."

"When did the wedding date change?" Jandro asked them. "And why wasn't I consulted? Despite the federal and state involvement, Grace Haven is our town, and our police force knows the nuts and bolts of this area far better than an outsider would."

Kim spoke up first. "We ran into site and

scheduling problems earlier this month," she told him.

"And once Rick became the official party candidate, Secret Service guidelines took precedence," Drew added.

"This would have been easier in a closed, single road venue," the lieutenant said. "With no lake view."

"Which kind of messes up the whole reason to have a beautiful Finger Lakes wedding, doesn't it?" Kimberly said. "It's a balancing act, for sure."

Jandro shifted his attention back to Drew. "Rick Vandeveld has friends who spend the summer here. He understands the social climate better than most. What is he prepared to do to offset this disruption in people's daily lives? It seems to me that other major weddings have offered neighbors a token of apology for inconveniencing them."

"Hosting the November Christkindl and the New Year's Eve fireworks would be a lovely tribute," Kimberly offered smoothly. "Those two events cost the town nearly thirty thousand in out-of-pocket expenses. To have the senator sponsor them will go a long way as a means of forgiveness. And overtime for the local force, of course."

"I concur." Jandro made a note and shifted

his attention to Drew. "Can you run that by the senator today? I can quietly schedule overtime to make sure we have a full contingent on hand, but the cost of that needs to be covered by the senator, not the town or the county."

"I'll talk with him today," Drew promised. He motioned to the site grid he'd brought in. "Everything else seems fine?"

"Yes. We'll notify the state troopers and the county sheriff, but I'll tell them not to share the actual information until we need to at the last minute."

"Perfect." Drew stood. "Lieutenant, I appreciate this."

The lieutenant frowned. "Well, there'll be backlash, but I think once people realize it's a onetime occurrence, they'll be okay. And then we're going to hope the next big wedding picks another lake to host it."

"But we don't want to overlook the upside of this wedding and events like this," Kimberly countered. "This wedding has dropped over one hundred and ten thousand dollars into our economy so far, without the senator's help on those events. And that's not including the guest lodgings at area B and B's, hotels and inns. If we can keep the stress of the road closings minimal, we could actually encourage this kind of event."

"A valid point," Jandro conceded. "I'll take

care of my end," he assured them before directing his attention toward Kimberly alone. "If you think of anything Mrs. Gonzalez or I can do to help out, let us know. I know you girls are running yourselves ragged over there..."

"We're fine," she assured him and gave him a big hug. "But thank you. And I'll keep it in mind. The bride might need to get out from under Drew's control at some point in time or go pre–wedding day ballistic. I might bring her into town to visit you and Dottie. She'd get a kick out of that."

She ignored Drew's glare as she left the room, and she got halfway across the parking lot before he caught up with her and grabbed her arm. "You're mad because I didn't include you on this meeting."

"I'm not mad." She turned and faced him full-on, and if anger had a color, it was there in her big blue eyes. "I'm furious. You made a big show of wanting to be in on everything concerning this wedding. I've tried to play by your rules, but when you leave next month, the rest of us still need to live here. And while one day may not seem like a lot to you guys, a day of no sales during the height of the busy season is a significant loss for people who live paycheck to paycheck."

She took a short breath and pointed at him, and her look of disappointment cut more than her words. "Before you pull any more side deals, let me remind you that we're supposed to be working together. And that hasn't happened for the last week. And FYI, Kate & Company has two weddings to oversee tomorrow, and then I'm taking the rest of Labor Day weekend off to clean out my mother's neglected gardens. I don't want to talk weddings or security or anything, got it? I'm going to throw on sweats and a T-shirt and get dirty because while the wheelers and dealers of Vandeveld Securities might hire this stuff done, we simple folks do it ourselves. When there's time."

She pivoted and walked away, shoulders back, head high.

He couldn't go after her. She'd want explanations, and he had none. Mistakes from the past left her brother dead. They weren't his mistakes. He understood that. But David wasn't any less dead because of them.

Drew covered all the bases now, always. Maybe too well, but he was okay with that, except when he saw the sheen of angry tears in her pretty blue eyes.

The rose garden weeds were the first to succumb.

Kimberly set up her mother's old radio, cranked up a country station and cleaned up those roses in quick order, and because she was already mad at the world, she almost welcomed the occasional prick of a thorn.

She ignored the pretty church bells, waved to a few neighbors who called hello as they walked to church and pretended her lack of attendance wasn't notable.

"Kimberly, do you want me to wait and go to the later service with you?" Rory came out of the kitchen door about the same time the slap of Drew's screen door announced his arrival outside. She ignored him and looked up at her sister.

"No, I'm good. Go on ahead."

"You're sure? Because I could help you here and then we can go together."

"Hey, Kimberly!" Amy's cheerful greeting forced her to turn, and when she did, she aimed her gaze at the excited preteen alone.

"Morning, sweet thing. Are you off to church?"

"Yes." Amy reached out and clasped her father's hand. "Do you want to go with us?"

"I'm praying in the garden today." She said the words casually, but regret poked her, making her think she *should* pray in the garden. What better place was there? If you believed in that sort of thing, of course.

"I've prayed in a few gardens myself," Drew admitted behind her.

She refused to look up or acknowledge him,

and when Rory fell into step beside them, Kimberly kept her attention firmly on dandelion removal. By the time they returned, laughing and easy, nearly two hours later, she'd weeded the front gardens and started shoveling mulch into the wheelbarrow.

Ten minutes later, two strong arms took the shovel out of her hands. "Hey!" She looked up, puffed a loose lock of sweaty hair out of her eyes and met Drew's gaze.

She didn't want to look into his eyes. She didn't want to be attracted to another man who ran hot and cold on whims. She wanted—

"I'll do this. The kid wants to help you, and there's not enough room for two people to shovel, so if you let her help out back, I'll do the mulching out here. Please."

Stubborn anger reared up, but she'd be stupid to refuse help, especially when the back gardens were ten times worse than the front. "Okay."

She handed off the shovel, but when she did, he placed one big, strong, gentle hand over hers. The warmth of his palm softened her angst like a lake breeze on a muggy afternoon.

She longed to move forward but forced herself backward.

She'd had enough of cops and cop types. She'd watched the sacrifices her mother made because of her father's job, she'd said goodbye to her brother far too soon and when she'd given another guy in uniform a chance, he'd dumped her. Steer clear of police was her new mantra, but temptation claimed her every time she came within ten feet of Drew Slade. She'd push that temptation aside, though, because she wanted and deserved honesty. Keeping her out of the loop on Shelby's wedding because he knew she wouldn't approve of certain things was too high-handed for Kimberly's tastes. No matter how good he looked escorting Amy to church, or now, shoveling mulch as if his life depended on it.

She moved toward the backyard. "Amy, come on over here. My mom's got more trowels and gloves in the garden shed."

"Gloves?" Amy cringed when she looked at the stained, used gloves. "I'll just use my hands, I think."

Kimberly laughed and shoved the gloves into her hands. "You'll use gloves if you want to help because poison ivy loves to poke through these shade gardens. Keep the gloves on, and don't scratch your face. And if you think you see some, I'll be glad to nip it out. I'm not allergic, but you might be."

"I am." Amy frowned at the used gloves but tugged them into place. "I got into some at camp last year. It was awful. Hey, isn't that Tee and her stupid brother?"

"It is." It was hard to argue the *stupid* adjective when the kid had been acting mean to Amy. "We're grilling hot dogs and hamburgers today. They're coming over to help with the yard work, and then we'll all eat and go swimming later, before the fireworks."

"Why is he such a jerk?" she asked as Callan stomped up the front sidewalk toward the front door of the house. "Being nice is so much easier."

It was, but it was a lesson Kimberly had to learn personally, so she cut Callan some slack. "He'll get over it."

"I hope so." Amy grabbed a trowel and started working from the back corner, forward, as far as she could get from Callan. Tee dashed out the back door a few minutes later, dressed to work. "Amy, let's work together!"

"Sweet." Amy grinned her way, and the two girls chattered like magpies as they weeded. Before too long, Kimberly glimpsed Patriot hostas surrounded by the waving fronds of bleeding hearts. By the time they'd had one lemonade break and a quick ham sandwich, half of the sloping, wide backyard was done.

"This is a lot of gardens."

She'd been ignoring Drew, kind of like Amy

was ignoring Callan, but when he came around back and whistled appreciation for their efforts, she swiped her sleeve across her forehead and nodded. "My mother claims this is satisfying labor. Personally, I'm finding nothing therapeutic about it."

"Anger management?" he suggested, and she wanted to smack him because he was almost right. She wasn't nearly as angry as she'd been, so maybe gardening was better therapy than homicide.

"In that case it might be considered a stress reliever," she conceded.

"I'll start mulching where the girls were working. Corinne invited us to eat with you guys tonight."

"You live right there, so it's kind of a given, isn't it?"

"I'm not assuming anything until you tell me I'm forgiven for not filling you in on everything," he said as he started laying down mulch. "I should have trusted your judgment."

"That's old news."

"Not until you forgive me, it isn't," he decided, and set to work filling the wheelbarrow again.

"Kimberly, I'm taking the kids for a swim." Corinne came out the back door a few minutes later. "Are you guys okay here?"

"We've got a radio and iced tea. We're good."

Corinne headed down the driveway toward the water. Amy and Tee walked off ahead of her, still talking. Callan dragged his feet behind, and when they got almost to the road, he turned abruptly, came back to the house and banged in the front door.

An awkward silence ensued between the two adults. Drew cast a look toward the house, as if wondering what to do.

Kimberly had no words of wisdom. Anger in a grown-up was tough enough. In a kid it became magnified by immaturity, an uneasy combination. They worked quietly until Drew leaned on the shovel, late in the day. "What time do the fireworks start tonight?"

"Around eight because it's dark by then. Why?"

"Rocky's not good with fireworks. He reacts as if there's gunfire. I'll make sure he's locked in the apartment."

"Can we take Amy down to the shore to see them?"

"She'll love it. She hasn't found anything about this town she doesn't love. Except maybe…" He directed his gaze toward the house, which meant Callan. "I'm hoping that will iron itself out in time."

Kimberly hoped so, too, but when Callan sullenly refused to go to the fireworks with them later, she wasn't any too sure. Emily thrust a blanket into her arms and grabbed a second one as they headed out the door. "Don't look back. He wants us to feel sorry for him."

"I kind of do," Kimberly whispered.

"Then you're a softie," Emily hissed back. "He's being a brat, and he knows better, so if he wants to sit here and mope, that's his choice."

Emily was right, Corinne seemed to agree, and Kimberly didn't want Drew and Amy to feel badly about the whole thing, but leaving Callan behind was hard.

"Toughen up," Corinne advised her as they crossed the road to the lakeside park. "Callan's got to learn to weigh his choices. I've talked 'til I'm blue in the face, and he's determined to put the loss of his father at Drew's door. And that's not fair."

"I know that firsthand," Kimberly replied. "But I still feel bad for him."

"I do, too, but my grandma had a great saying, one I keep handy at times like this. She said, 'Better they cry now than you cry later.'"

"Tough love. I get it. But when he looks up at me with his daddy's eyes, I go to mush." They settled their blankets along the slope of the east-facing hill. Figures dashed back and forth as kids lit the night with sparklers and glow sticks. Campfires along the beach were set up to toast marshmallows or build s'mores. After Kimberly set their bag of marshmallows down on the nearest picnic table and turned around, the only spot on a blanket was directly in front of the table, next to Drew. Her sisters and Corinne had not so innocently taken up the first blanket, which meant she could either sit on the damp ground, the chilly picnic bench or the dry blanket.

Next to Drew.

The blanket won. She sat on one side, nearest her family, leaving space for Amy and Tee, but the girls had joined the crowd of kids around the first dock.

Drew leaned back, gazing up, studying the stars. "It's a perfect night."

It was. The heat had dissipated, leaving cool, fresh air to bathe her skin, enough to need a sweater or hoodie. And her mother's gardens were done, so that made the evening even better.

"Stars. Moon. Fireworks."

It was a recipe for romance, or could have been. Regret hit her as she remembered that kiss. She'd thought—no, hoped—that there was something special between her and Drew, but she'd mistaken attraction for true affection.

That was her mistake, and not one she was likely to make again. Darkness settled in, deepening the shadows. When the first round of fireworks went off, the crowd exclaimed in appreciation. Volley after volley lit the night, and the thunderous follow-ups boomed through the air.

"Amazing, isn't it?" Drew spoke softly, but it wasn't the fireworks he was watching. It was Tee and Amy, laughing and hugging each other, feminine versions of their fathers.

"Time marches on." She kept her voice soft, too, beneath the noise surrounding them. "They're wonderful girls."

"Listen, Kimberly—"

She shook her head and held up a hand to stop him, but he didn't stop. He sat more upright and faced her. "I know you don't want to hear this, but it's important. I get a little overbearing when it comes to Rick and his family—"

"A little?"

"More than a little," he conceded. "But I owe them. I owe him. And with all that's happened this past year, the changes we're all going to face because of his candidacy, I wanted this wedding perfectly safe. It's my way of thanking him for believing in a stupid drunk a bunch of years back."

Her heart softened.

Atonement was something she understood well, because she'd been a jerk about Dave's death for years. "I hear you."

"I'll back off," he promised, facing forward,

keeping his eyes trained on the beautiful night before them. "Everything is done. All plans are made. We're down to implementation, and that means I've got two weeks of relative tranquility on my hands. That will probably drive me crazy, but I'm going to try to keep busy while staying calm and cool. Okay?"

It was okay, and his words offered deeper insight. Making sure this wedding went off without a hitch was repayment, and she'd help make that happen because it was a concept she understood. She was about to speak when a deep-throated bark sounded in the distance behind them. The bark grew louder, closer and more insistent, while the next batch of fireworks claimed the night.

But not for Drew. He was on his feet instantly and running back, toward the house.

Rocky.

She stood up and followed him. The sound of the big dog's agitated bark grew closer, and then the long, screaming screech of car brakes split the night.

And when the gut-wrenching thud said the car couldn't come to a stop in time, fear and adrenaline pushed her to run faster.

She raced the last hundred feet and came to a quick stop at the curb. Drew, on his knees, bent low over his beloved friend, crooning words of comfort to the stricken shepherd. For just a moment, emotion threatened to claim her, but seeing Drew's heartbroken face, she couldn't give in.

Help him.

She clamped down the welling sympathy as she raced to his side. "Is he alive?"

"Barely."

"I'll get the car." She didn't pause for breath as she ran up to the house, crashed through the door, grabbed the car keys and brought the SUV down the driveway to the road's edge.

People had circled around, their backs to the fireworks, saddened by the tragedy marring the day. Jandro Gonzalez and Bob Gunther helped Drew lift the big dog into the back of the vehicle. Drew climbed in after him. "Can you drive?" He looked at Kimberly, and the pain in his eyes stumbled her resolve, but she tucked Amy into the passenger seat and headed north, toward the emergency veterinary clinic.

In the space of a minute, everything had changed, but there was an extra heavy burden weighing on Kimberly's shoulders as she drove.

She'd seen Callan's face as she ran into the house. She'd passed him on the curving driveway, and the look on his face said guilty as charged, which meant Callan had some serious reckoning ahead of him.

Had he released Rocky from the apartment? Gone in to see the dog?

She didn't know, and right now she needed to focus her attention on Drew, Amy and the beautiful shepherd who took his job and his family seriously. *Take care of him, God. Them. Please. And please don't let Rocky die.*

She'd called ahead to the veterinary ER, and a crew rushed a gurney to the back of the car as soon as she pulled in. They bundled Rocky onto it, applied the restraints and had him whisked into the depths of triage before Drew could get inside to give his name.

"Will he die?" Amy whispered, clinging to Kimberly's side.

What answer could Kimberly give? She made a face and hugged the girl tighter. "I don't know. But we can pray for him, can't we?"

Amy bit down hard on her lip and nodded. She dipped her chin, praying silently, and the sight of this tough, precocious girl facing another loss broke Kimberly's heart. She wanted to crumble, but another part of her longed to help Amy face whatever loomed ahead. She snugged her arm around the girl and prayed with her while Drew gave the receptionist the information she needed.

And when he turned, his pallor made her want to help him, too. Her former misconceptions disappeared in the space of a heartbeat. This man—

her brother's partner and friend—had suffered a grievous loss when Dave died, and she'd been wrong and foolish to blame him, or think he didn't care because the grief-stricken man before her cared a great deal.

But when he caught sight of Amy's sorrow, he calmed his gaze and moved their way with the face she'd seen at Dave's funeral. Not *him*, not the real Drew, a man of deep emotion, but the face he laid carefully in place to help others in their time of need.

"Hey." He stooped low and took Amy into his arms while blinking back moisture in his eyes. "You praying?"

"Yes, sir."

"Me, too."

She looked up at him, wanting reassurance, but read her father's gaze and took a deep breath. "I don't want to lose any part of Team Slade."

"Me, either."

Amy nodded, hugged him, then settled back into the chair, trying to be brave. "So we pray and put him in God's hands."

"Every day," Drew assured her, and took the seat on her other side. He took her right hand in his left and bowed his head, and the two of them sat, linked by hand and faith.

Kimberly swallowed hard.

Prayer came easy when she was young. And

then she'd moved away, gotten busy, shrugged off church, time, prayer and God as if none of it was important.

Of course it was. Why had she been so stupid?

She kept Amy's left hand lightly in her own, and joined with them in silent prayer.

The door swung open across from them.

Corinne came in with Callan.

Drew looked up, and Kimberly watched as realization turned his expression to resignation. Somehow, reading Callan's face and posture, he knew.

Corinne drew Callan closer. "How's Rocky?"

Drew shook his head. "He's badly injured. We don't know anything yet."

She turned toward Callan and thrust him forward. "Tell him."

Kimberly wasn't sure this was the right time or place, but she'd also figured out that parenting wasn't a walk in the park. Corinne seemed to handle it with a strength Kimberly respected.

Drew didn't stand. He sat, Amy's hand tucked in his, and faced the boy.

"I let him out."

Drew's color faded. "Why would you do that?"

Callan cringed, not daring to look Drew or Amy in the eye. "I wanted to see him. Meet him. I didn't know he wouldn't stay right there—I thought a police dog would just listen to everything I said. Like he does with you. I'm so sorry."

Kimberly had been watching Drew, so when Amy hurled herself out of the chair, she sat back, surprised.

"You stupid jerk!" Amy yelled, and when Callan took a step back, she followed. "You're a jerk to me, and a jerk to my dad and now you might have killed Rocky! I hate you!"

"Amy." Drew reached out to tug her back, into his arms, but she whirled out of reach.

Callan shrank back, as surprised as anyone; then he turned and ran out of the waiting room, into the night.

Corinne went after him, Drew grabbed Amy and Kimberly sat still, shocked into reality for the second time in less than an hour.

Should she go after Corinne and Callan? Or stay here with Drew and Amy?

A plaque on the far wall gained her attention, Coleridge's words of wisdom for all to see. "He prayeth best, who loveth best / All things great and small / For the dear God who loveth us / He made and loveth all." A box of Golden Retriever pups peeked up between the vintage reminder, their wide blue eyes excited to climb out of the box, examine the world around them.

She'd seen the anguish in Callan's face, heard

it in his voice, but he'd set the stage for Amy's reaction with his continued bad behavior.

How could Drew and Amy ever forgive him? And how quickly could one event change a boy's life?

"I'll talk to him when things calm down. When we know more," Drew added.

She turned and saw that Amy had climbed into her father's lap. For this moment the rugged tomboy adventurer had turned back into Daddy's little girl, and the sweetness of that melted her heart.

"Mr. Slade?"

"Yes." Drew stood and carefully set Amy down at his side. "How is he?"

"He's in surgery. We're lucky that the car missed full body impact, but he's got a long recovery ahead of him. The damage is mostly to his hindquarters. I'll have a more detailed list available later, but the operating doctor wants you to know he's optimistic."

A rush of thankfulness flooded Kimberly. She reached over and grasped Amy's hand. "You think he's going to be okay?"

"I do. He'll need time, rest and daily care, but yes. We think so."

Kimberly wasn't sure who grabbed who first, but she found herself hugging Amy and hugging

Drew, and he was hugging both of them, as well. "Should we stay, Doctor?"

The doctor shrugged. "That's up to you. You won't be able to see him until tomorrow. The surgery is going to take a while because of the amount of damage incurred, and if there's any change in Rocky's condition, I'll call you right away. I'm on all night, so I'll be with him throughout. I'm Dr. Towner, by the way."

"Can we stay, Dad?" Amy peered up at Drew and grasped his sleeves. "At least until his surgery is over? Like you'd do for me if I got hurt?"

"Absolutely." Drew reached out and shook the doctor's hand. "Thank you, Dr. Towner. We'll stay. Then I'll take this one home to bed because it looks like our September isn't going to be as laid-back as I thought a few hours ago. And that's all right, as long as Rocky's going to be okay."

The doctor went back to the surgical wing, and they retook their seats along the wall in the now-quiet waiting room.

Kimberly took stock of the past couple of hours.

They'd run the gamut, from highs to lows, but things could still come out all right. No matter what happened in the next few weeks, she'd realized something tonight.

It felt right to share the ups and downs of life

with Drew and Amy. As if she belonged there, with them. A part of them.

Admit it. You've fallen head over heels for this guy again. Be honest with yourself—you loved him as a starstruck kid. Maybe you always have?

Unlike Drew's, her September schedule was crazy busy, but if Drew and Amy needed her to help with Rocky or baseball or talking girl stuff to an inquisitive eleven-year-old, she'd do it because somehow, someway, she knew that's where God wanted her to be.

Chapter Thirteen

Jandro Gonzalez stopped by Drew's apartment on Labor Day morning. "How's Rocky doing? Any word?"

Drew stepped outside and pulled the door shut behind him so Amy could sleep in. "Nothing further except that he did well during surgery and is expected to recover."

"That's good to hear." Jandro clapped him on the shoulder, relieved. "We received your application for the chief's job, and it's going through the usual channels. I wanted to thank you for sending it in."

He'd followed through and done it, but now, with this latest bend in the road, did he have the right to stay in Grace Haven and possibly mess up Callan's life?

Maybe not, but that wasn't something he could discuss with the lieutenant commander. "I'm grateful for the chance, of course. And Pete's recommendation."

"Pete doesn't offer kudos lightly. Never did. But he's firmly in your corner, and with the work you've done downstate, the council would be foolish to pick someone else."

"And town councils never act foolishly, of course."

Jandro's wince said otherwise, but he waved as he moved toward his car. "Keep me updated on Rocky's condition. It's a shame to have something like that happen."

It was, and Drew knew he'd have to face Callan this morning. That wouldn't be easy for either of them.

Kimberly came out of the house with two mugs, and the sight of her, bringing him coffee, hinted of sweet possibilities. "Please tell me one of those is mine."

"This one." She held up her right hand and handed him the mug. "Any word?"

Drew's phone buzzed just then. He took the call with his free hand, and smiled at Kimberly. "He's doing okay, as expected, no surprises."

"I'm so glad." She set her coffee down on the picnic table and hugged him, and when he returned the favor, he realized how wonderful it would be to share this woman's life and love for the rest of his days. Being with Kimberly felt good and right, when she wasn't reaming him out over something, of course, but even that seemed delightfully normal, because that was Kimberly. Strong, assertive and a little bossy. Like him.

"I like hugging you," he whispered. She tried to pull back, and he laughed and snugged her closer. "Ten seconds more, okay? Then I can get through today."

She hugged him for longer than ten seconds, then moved back. "You're going to see Callan?"

"Yes." He took a long drink of coffee. "Do you mind keeping an eye on Amy for me?"

"Glad to. We were thinking of putting all the summer stuff away and putting the boat in storage. It's early, but I don't see when we'll have time to do it later on, and once the weather changes, it's a lot more work. And with Dad not here…" Her voice trailed off, and Drew understood. Things were different with Kate and Pete so far away.

"Amy would love a fall boat ride."

"She would, wouldn't she?" Kim swept the lake a glance. "But with school and her fall baseball league and homework, will there be time before Shelby's wedding? And after the wedding, you'll be gone."

Did she choke up just a little?

She did, and then she turned away to cover it up.

"Will you miss me? Us?" He looked toward the carriage house apartment behind him.

"Yes. Jerk."

He laughed, then sighed. "It should be easy, shouldn't it? You meet someone, fall in love and live the prescribed happily-ever-after you see on every princess movie known to man."

"In those scenarios, the prince is crazy rich. All he has to do is have his minions run the kingdom—"

"And slay the occasional dragon."

"I'll grant you that," she noted. "But essentially, other than the dragon killing, the prince isn't bogged down by life in the movies. Real life is a whole different thing."

"Well." He drank the rest of the coffee and moved toward the car. "I'm going over there now. Waiting only makes it worse."

"Bless you."

She said it as if wishing she could help him, and she *was* helping him by watching Amy. Facing Dave's son and dealing with years of deep-seated anger was all on him. He climbed into the car, backed around and headed west toward the small cape-style house Dave and Corinne had bought years before. And on the way, he prayed for the right words and that this meeting wouldn't make things worse. At this moment, he wasn't sure they could get worse.

Kimberly saw her mother's number and picked up the house phone. "Hey, Mom. What's up? It's morning. Is everything okay?"

"It's me, Kimber."

"Dad." Kimberly sank into a kitchen chair and motioned Emily and Rory to come over. "Hey, can you hear me okay if I put you on speaker? Em and Rory are right here."

"I'd like that."

Flanked by her sisters, she hit the speaker button. "Okay, Dad. We're all here."

"First, there's no emergency."

The girls exchanged a look of relief because if Dad was talking cop talk, he was doing all right.

"So you just called because you miss us, right?" Rory teased. "Or to see if the roof's leaking, gutters have been cleaned, lawn mowed et cetera because you know who does all that stuff around here. Surprisingly, your daughters have risen to the task, and, aside from roof stuff, all is well."

"You're amazing!" piped their mother's voice from the background. "I'm so proud of you girls!"

"Well, if you're that proud, stop sugarcoating things for us," Emily answered smoothly.

"I got thrown overboard by my supposed-to-be-forever husband. I'm doing a real good job here, according to my bossy big sister, and I've survived nicely. Therefore, you and Dad need to be straight with me and Rory, all the time. Got it?"

Pete laughed, and it sounded so good, so normal to hear him laugh at their mother. "They've got your number, Kate. All right, I'll reinforce your dictate here—I promise. But that's not why I called."

"Okay, Dad." Kimberly softened her tone. "It's your turn."

"I'm leaving the force."

Their dad hadn't planned to retire for at least another five years. "You're retiring? For sure?"

"Yes. And not because I'm sick right now, although that's been a wake-up call. I realized that your mother and I haven't had time alone in three decades. Time to just be. To travel. To meet new people. There's something real comfortable about Grace Haven, and it will be a great place to come home to, but if I get through this treatment all right, then I want to see some things before God calls me home. And if I don't come out all right, I still want to see some things, but I wanted you girls to know first."

"So..." Kimberly picked her words carefully. "Does that mean Mom's retiring, too?"

"Yes."

The girls exchanged looks of wonder.

"What about Kate & Company? Is there a plan?"

"Well, that depends on you girls," Pete answered smoothly. "Your mother worked hard to build that business, and it's brought us a lot of joy and a lot of income, but if it's not what any of you want to do with your lives, Mom will either sell it or close it once the current commitments are made."

Close the business.

Kimberly couldn't imagine such a thing; Kate & Company had been a mainstay in the town for decades. And yet...

Did she want to stay in Grace Haven and run the business? Did Emily?

One look at Rory's face said she wasn't interested. "Well, that's amazing news." She half croaked the reply, and her father's reassuring laugh said he understood.

"I wanted to call today because I want to go into this procedure knowing I've got everything taken care of."

Tightness grabbed Kimberly's throat. Her father was taking care of business today because he wasn't sure if he'd be around—or cognitive enough—to take care of things in the future.

"That's perfect timing, Dad." Rory jumped in

to save the moment. "We're going to pray you and that surgeon right through this."

One way or another this surgery would launch a new chapter for the Gallagher family. Instead of plunging into the unknown, their father was taking steps to ease the transition, no matter what happened.

"Dad, you guys have given us a lot to think about and pray over, and I expect you've got a few more phone calls to make," Emily added.

"I do, honey, but you guys needed to be brought on board first. And..." This time it was his voice that choked. "I love you, girls. Every one of you. You and your brother are the best things that ever happened to Mom and me, and I just wanted you to know that."

Worry shook Pete Gallagher's voice.

The girls exchanged concerned looks.

Kimberly refused to think that he might not be here. They'd gone to Houston for a cure, and that's what she intended to focus on. "Stay in touch as things happen, but, Dad, I totally believe you're going to be just fine." It took all her strength to pull out her tough, pragmatic voice, but she did it. "We're going to let you go so Emily and I can decide who gets Mom's business in a tug-of-war. I'm bigger, so I expect to win."

She winked at Emily as they hung up the

phone, but then all three girls sat, staring, wondering what the future would bring.

"Well." Rory stood up and dusted her hands together. "The new school year starts in forty-eight hours, and I've got kids to prep for. You've got to keep Amy busy once she's up, and Emily said she wanted to organize Mom's computer files."

"They are a mess," Kimberly agreed. "I spend way too much time searching for names and then opening and closing files to figure out which one I want. If you can make that easier, that would be a wonderful thing."

"I can and will." Emily heaved a breath, still looking at the phone. "And it's a nice quiet job that lets me pray the whole while. If you need me, guys, I'll be over in the office."

"Em?"

"Hmm?" She turned, read Kimberly's look and shrugged. "We'll figure out what to do with the business once we know what we're dealing with concerning Dad and Mom. Because while none of us wants to face the possibility of Dad not being here, what if he doesn't make it through? Would Mom still want to give up the business she loves and travel places alone?"

She made an excellent point. Kimberly shook her head. "No."

"So we wait. And because neither one of us

has a host of other offers sitting on the table, it's okay to take some time."

"Agreed." The slap of Drew's screen door indicated Amy was awake. "I'm going to go tell a cute kid her dog's doing all right, and maybe they'll let us visit him." She met Amy halfway up the walk and hugged her. "Rocky's holding his own, he's in stable condition, and the vet is pleased with these first postsurgical twelve hours."

"Oh, that's good news!" Amy hugged her back, relieved. "Where's Dad?"

Kimberly didn't mince words. "He went to see Callan." When Amy drew back and scowled, Kimberly bent down to her level. "How old were you when your mother died?"

Amy rolled her eyes, but her features relaxed slightly. "Three."

"Do you remember her?"

"Almost." She took a deep breath and sighed. "No. I remember pictures of her, but it's like she was never even there."

"Then maybe you can understand Callan a little better," Kimberly reasoned. "He was just a toddler when his father was killed. For him, meeting your dad must have brought back a lot of old feelings. I'm not excusing his behavior," she added firmly. "But it can be a tough thing to handle when life blindsides you."

"So he gets to hate us forever? Because that's just plain wrong."

"It's not you he hates. Or your father, really. It's circumstances, honey. And that's a part of growing up that's tough to figure out. Hey, you hungry?"

Amy shook her head. "I want to go see Rocky, if we can."

"I'll call and ask right now." She made the call as they entered the kitchen, then hung up the phone. "They said we can come by later as long as he's okay. He's sleeping now and rest is important for healing."

"And they probably don't want us to get him all excited," Amy noted. "K-9 partners want to work. When they see their partners, the first thing they want to do is get back on the job."

"Sounds like Rocky's perfect for your dad," Rory said as she came into the kitchen. "Two hardworkin' guys, gettin' it done."

"That's them all right."

Rory popped bread into the toaster and as the smell of warm yeast filled the air, she waited a few seconds, then turned back toward Amy. "This is my favorite bread in the world—it makes the most perfect toast ever. Want some?"

Amy had said no to food outside, but Rory had tempted her senses with the sweet scent of toasting bread. She nodded and slipped into a chair at the table. "It smells really good."

"And with fresh butter and Mom's homemade cherry jam, it's the most delicious food known to man," Rory continued, and Kimberly had to hand it to her. Her younger sister knew her way around kids, big and small.

Mags dashed into the room, sniffed Amy and sat back, then raced to the door, feet braced, expecting to hear or see Rocky outside. And when she didn't, the little dog sat down hard on her hindquarters, as if she was disappointed.

"Do you think…" Kimberly paused the question and looked at Rory and Amy.

"She misses him?" Rory finished the thought, surprised. "No way."

"She hates him," breathed Amy, but she took the first piece of toast over to the door and swung the door open to let Mags out.

Mags studied the terrain from inside the kitchen, then sighed, flopped down and pouted.

"She doesn't hate him," Kimberly decided. "She likes him. She likes having a sparring partner around."

"Remind you of anyone?" Rory asked under her breath, and when Kimberly faced her, Rory grinned. "They say dogs are a lot like their owners. You could be proving science right."

"Hush up," Kimberly scolded, but she couldn't deny the analogy between her and Drew.

"Aw, Mags." Amy bent low and petted the silky little dog. "He'll be back soon. I promise."

Two thumps of Mags's tail said she'd wait, and that's exactly what she did. Each time they went in and out the back door, the little dog sat up, studied the backyard, then sat back down, determined.

By late morning, Mags's antics had proved their theory. She wanted her big dog friend back, and she had no intention of playing with anyone or anything until Rocky returned.

"It's kind of weird, isn't it?" Amy asked when she climbed into the car just after lunch. The vet hospital had given them the green light to come visit Rocky. "How sad would it be if she waited and waited and he didn't come back?"

"Kind of like you and Callan. You both woke up one day to a new reality. And you're doing all right."

Amy's lower lip pushed out. "How do dogs and kids understand these things? Because even though it was a long time ago, there's a little part of me that wishes my mom would come walking through a door someday and say, 'Hey, Amy! It's all a mistake. I'm home!'"

"Oh, honey, no one understands these things.

We just square our shoulders, pray and move on. And after a while it's not so raw."

"You think I should forgive Callan."

"Of course you should." Never one to pull punches, Kimberly gave it to her directly, mostly because she'd made the same mistake personally. "Forgiveness is the key to everything. Going through life carrying grudges isn't good for anyone. It took me a while to figure that out. I'd like to see you grasp the concept more quickly."

Amy flashed her a little smile. "Tee's mom did say you and Callan were a lot alike."

"Which is why I'd like to see him happy, too. He's my nephew, and I love him. Maybe he can learn the lesson quicker than I did." She pointed ahead. "Your dad's pulling in ahead of us."

"I see him!" Amy was out of her seat belt and across the parking area quickly. She hugged her father tightly, and in her face Kimberly saw the joy of morning. Rocky was going to be okay, and seeds of forgiveness had lightened the girl's expression.

But when Drew lifted wounded eyes to hers, a warning knell sounded. His gaze said it hadn't gone well with Callan.

She moved closer and clasped his hand because right then, no matter what the future held, Drew looked as though he needed a friend.

He gripped her fingers tight, then slung an easy arm around Amy's shoulders. "Let's do this."

"We have to stay calm, Dad," Amy cautioned as they reentered the waiting area of the clinic. "We don't want to get him all excited."

"I'll keep it down," Drew promised. He flashed a smile to Kimberly, but she read the pain behind the smile and realized she'd seen that look before. She just hadn't recognized it. It was the look she saw on Drew's face after Dave was killed, an expression that said he'd deal with the here and now as best he could…

And then he'd quietly slip away, alone with his personal dragons.

She didn't want that to happen again, but how did one fix a coiled rope of knotted dreams?

One loop at a time.

The thought came to her like a breath of wind, sweet and calm.

When you uncoil the knotted middle, you always find a beginning and an end.

Drew's words, from so long ago, as true now as they were then.

She walked with them into the recovery area, and knew what she needed to do. Piece by piece she needed to iron out the fabric of their lives. She might not be able to fix everything, but she had the ability to change certain things, and with that in mind, she called Corinne later that afternoon and set a plan in motion.

One way or another, she wasn't going to let Drew and Amy leave town with more guilt laid at his doorstep. He'd paid too high a price already.

Jesus had talked a lot about forgiveness.

For a time, Kimberly had forgotten to listen.

Well, she was listening now and for the next few weeks, Kimberly planned on doing everything she could to smooth out the kinks in their lives. It might not fix everything, but at this point, it couldn't possibly get worse.

Chapter Fourteen

"Dad, I can stay with you." Amy planted her feet in front of Rocky's big metal kennel late Wednesday afternoon and folded her arms. "We can't leave Rocky alone, and I can play baseball anytime." Her first day of school had gone well, and Kimberly had even taken her on an impromptu shopping trip for a few outfits.

"Not with Coach Cutler," Drew reminded her. "And you made a commitment, Amy. I'm just sorry I can't be there to see you, but Kimberly and Emily are going. And Tee will be there with her mom."

"Sir?"

Drew turned toward the first garage bay. Rocky couldn't make it up the stairs to the second-story apartment, so they'd set up his kennel here on the carriage house floor. He stared at Callan, surprised, then approached him slowly. "Yes?"

"I've come to stay with the dog." Callan pointed toward Rocky's cage. "With Rocky. While you guys go to the game."

"But you're playing," Drew said, stalling to assess this new wrinkle. "So that can't exactly work."

"I'm not." Callan sucked in a deep breath, rolled his baseball cap around in his hands and frowned. "I talked to Coach, and he gave me a leave as long as Rocky needs someone to watch him. It was my fault that he got hurt, and you shouldn't have to miss the games because of something I did."

Drew was about to argue when Amy took a cautious step forward. "You'd give up playing to help us?"

Callan sent her an awkward look. "Well. I did it. And it was a dumb thing to do."

"Dad?" Amy peered up at him. "What do you think?"

He liked the noble gesture, it spoke well of the boy, but he couldn't look at Callan's sad eyes without wanting to roll back the years and bring back Dave. And while that wasn't possible, he realized that every time Callan saw him, the boy was reminded of what he'd lost. That didn't seem right, which meant Drew and Amy had to leave right after the wedding. Even if the town council offered him the job.

He was about to wave the boy off when Kimberly strolled across the drive. "It's a perfect solution." She pointed to the SUV. "Let's go or the kid will be late and Coach will have her running laps."

"Right." Amy tugged Drew's hand toward the car.

"Does he need to go out or anything? Or is he okay to just be in his kennel?"

"He was just out for a few minutes, so he'll probably sleep for the evening."

"Okay." Callan pulled up a lawn chair, then produced a book from his jacket pocket.

"Have you started it yet?" Amy paused before climbing in the car and looked at the book.

Callan shook his head. "We just got it today, remember?"

"I read it last year, in Jersey. It's a great story."

"You gonna read it again?" His expression said reading it once was punishment enough, and Amy laughed.

"Yes. I loved it. Thanks for staying with Rocky."

"Yeah. Well." He looked down and around, anywhere but at them, embarrassed. "Good luck tonight."

"If we ever get there." Kimberly pointed to her wrist as if she wore a watch. "Clock's ticking, guys. Let's go."

"Callan."

The boy looked up and met Drew's gaze.

"Have you got a phone?"

He shook his head but pointed to the main house. "If anything happens, I'll call Mom from the house phone."

"All right." Drew climbed into the passenger seat, opened the window and drummed his fingers on the roof of the car as they pulled away.

"They'll both be fine." Kimberly made the turn west and then paused at the crossroads for a red light. "Consider it therapy."

"For whom?"

"All of you," she told him, and when she flashed him a smile that called his bluff, he sighed.

"I didn't want to leave him there."

"Really, Captain Obvious?"

He flushed. "But you're right, it was the best thing to do."

"Amy, do you have a pen?"

"No, why?"

Kim pretended to frown. "So we can write that down. Your father said I was right."

Amy played along nicely. "A rare occasion in the Slade house."

"I've noticed."

"I'll pencil it in when we get home," she promised, laughing.

"Thank you."

"Hey. Knock it off, you two." Drew aimed a fierce look at Amy that she'd learned to brush off years before. "I pay compliments as deserved."

"Then it might behoove you to think about paying them more as needed than deserved," Kimberly noted lightly. "We catch more flies with honey than vinegar."

"This is Kimberly Gallagher talking?"

She flashed him a quick smile, a smile he'd looked forward to every day since coming back to Grace Haven. "Let's just say I'm turning a new page and ready to operate on the more sunny side of life."

"You're scaring me." He winked at Amy, but he couldn't deny that something about Kimberly seemed different. Less angry and more focused. "What brought this on? Is your dad doing okay?"

"He's doing fine, they have the procedure scheduled for next Monday and then we'll move forward."

He climbed out of the car once she parked and met her gaze across the roof as Amy dashed off to join the team in warm-ups. "I like this new page. It's positively cheerful."

"Do you?" She rounded the hood of the car and faced him. "Because you could use a dose of cheerful yourself, Andrew."

He held up his hands and backed up a step.

"You mean well, Kimber, but save your lecture, okay? I never expected to come back here. Who would have thought Shelby would pick my hometown to have her wedding? She did, and I'm here, but you saw Callan tonight. Every time the kid sees me, he misses his father more. That's a rotten thing to do to anyone."

"We all have things to deal with." She held his gaze like she always did, never backing down, and he realized that was part of the allure. Kimberly took charge, like he did. She grabbed hold and hung on, just like him. She met him step for step, and he loved that about her. "We can't deal with them effectively if we run again. You and I tried that already. I do believe it was a bust."

"It's not running," he corrected her softly. "It's sacrificing one thing for another. Dave's son deserves to have a wonderful childhood, just like Amy. I can't in good conscience thrust that boy into a situation I'd hate for my own daughter. It's as simple as that."

He thought she'd commiserate. Share his feelings. Understand and empathize. But this was Kimberly, and she leaned forward and kissed him sweetly, then tweaked his hat. "Let's go watch a ball game. And buy me popcorn. I'm starving."

Watch a ball game?

Buy popcorn?

Was she serious? He'd just laid his selfless heart before her, and she wanted food?

But as they drew closer to the field the smell of fresh-popped corn *was* enticing, so he ordered three buckets to share, overpaid Bertie Engle again and found a seat next to Kimberly in the bleachers.

And it felt good, which felt wrong because Dave's kid wasn't playing. He was home, watching a dog, sacrificing his fall ball games to try and fix things.

Atonement.

You get that, better than most, don't you? Aren't you fussing over this wedding like a crazy man to show Rick how much his confidence and friendship has meant to you?

The kid needs atonement to help him heal, just like you.

"You're overthinking something again." Corinne smacked his leg from the seat below him. "Knock it off, Slade. Got it?"

"There is something seriously mean going on with the women in this town," he growled, rubbing his leg before passing her a tub of popcorn. "What happened to sweet, affable, easygoing girls? Because that might be a welcome change right about now."

Corinne waved him off, and Kimberly bumped shoulders with him. "They're a dime a dozen.

We like our local gals to be strong enough to be gentle and play a mean game of catch. Like that second baseman out there."

He followed the direction of her gaze toward Amy, and he had to admit she fit the profile. Strong, tough, engaging, precocious and growing more self-assured by the day.

She loves it here. She's at home here. Do you really want to drag her away from all this if the town extends an offer?

He didn't want to, no. But he needed to, and that made all the difference.

Kimberly made it a point to stroll slowly down the stone-paved walk on Sunday morning, and every measured step was worth it when Drew stepped outside and saw her. Appreciation quickened his gaze, and his smile grew as he held the screen door wide for Amy. "I think we've got company, kid."

"Kimberly!" Amy grinned and high-fived her. "I'm so glad you're coming and that it's nice out so we can walk. It was cold last night."

"We're heading into the change of seasons," Kimberly agreed. "We turn a lot of weather pages in the fall around here. It pays to keep the sweaters handy, that's for sure."

Amy almost frowned, then firmed her chin, stoic. "I like that stuff. The weather changes and the trees starting to turn colors. But—" she looked up at her dad and clasped his hand "—whatever Dad decides is okay as long as we're together."

"Team maintenance," Kimberly replied, smiling as they headed down the driveway.

"You know people will talk if you come to church with us." Drew reminded her as they drew near Center Street.

"Did they talk when my sister went with you?"

"No."

"Then—"

"This is different."

It was. She knew that, but it was nice to hear him recognize it. "Dad's surgery is tomorrow."

He nodded, reached out and clasped her hand with his free one. "Reason enough to pray right there."

"Yes. But there are other important things to think about and pray about now, too." She squeezed his hand lightly, a message meant just for him. "I feel like we're coming to an intersection with too many choices, none of them well marked. That would have made me mad a few months ago. It did make me mad," she admitted. "But then I stepped back and checked out the possibilities, and I'm okay with taking things more slowly. Making each choice count."

"Living deliberately."

She accepted his words and nodded. "Good way of putting it. I can't change certain things, but if I stay focused, I can make other things better for people. And that's what I've decided to do."

"You thinking of staying, Kimber? Permanently?"

"I *am* staying. No matter what Nashville might offer. I like being home."

He stopped and held her gaze, and the regret in his eyes said way more than his words. "I think it's a good decision."

"It is. And I hear there are plenty of other opportunities here. For the right people, that is."

Drew frowned. "Someone is talking too much."

"That someone is my father, and he's allowed to talk," she scolded. "And he only told us girls about his recommendation after he explained about his retirement. So your secret is safe with us. But I won't deny that gives me an additional focus at church this morning."

"Which would be fine if it was just me we were talking about. But it's not."

She didn't pursue the thought because she knew Drew. He'd weigh things up on his own and make the best decision he could based on facts, a cop at heart. But if she could tip the scales in favor of staying here, with her?

She'd do it.

He didn't let go of her hand when they climbed the church steps. Or when they walked inside. And when they picked a seat on the left, near the middle, he let Amy and her go in first, always the gentleman.

Heads turned. Folks smiled. Some waved and nodded, and she'd known this would happen if they strolled into church together as if she was part of Team Slade. Right then, it felt as if she was.

She wouldn't tug and twist on Drew's heart because she understood regret, just like him. But if God decided to put a little pressure on the rugged security man to stay put and see what developed, she'd be okay with that.

Kimberly braced for backlash when Jandro and the mayor had the road-closed notices hand-delivered to neighbors and affected businesses on Sunday afternoon, but aside from a handful of grumbles, the feedback was positive.

"Mrs. Hanning wants us to know she's pleased to do her part for the wedding by staying home, which is exactly what she would have done anyway, and her sister said having the senator's daughter get married in the Abbey puts it in the history books. And she'd like a slice of the chocolate strawberry groom's cake, if at all possible."

"What a great thought," Emily agreed from her desk. "To have the wedding vendors sweeten the pot for the neighbors is smart business. I'll get right on that, if it's all right with you, Kimber?"

"It's an excellent idea," Kimberly answered from the wall-size planning board where she and Allison were doing one last visual of the final seating arrangements. Her burner phone rang. Drew's number appeared in the display. She picked it up and moved down the hall so her conversation wouldn't interrupt Emily and Allison as they rechecked each detail of a five-day itinerary. "Are you off to the airport?"

"I am. I'm bringing security teams into town. They'll look like average citizens and tourists, and they'll be everywhere. Call me as soon as you hear about your father's surgery, okay?"

"I will," Kimberly promised. "It won't be until later with the time difference and all, but I'll call."

"All right. And, Kimber?"

His voice hesitated as if weighing what to say.

"Yes?"

He hesitated, and while Drew Slade appeared stoic and unemotional on the surface, Kimberly read the anxiety within him. "Aw, don't go getting all sentimental on me, Slade. We've got work to do, and I have a bride—and her mother—arriving tomorrow afternoon. And they may or may not approve weeks of nonstop work. For you and me, this week is pure focus. We're leaving the rest to God."

It felt good to hear him laugh and agree. "You're absolutely right, I'll talk to you later."

"Good. Love you."

The moment crunched to a swift stop, and for the life of her, she couldn't imagine why those last two words had slipped out.

Sure you can.

Well, okay, she could, but—

"You waited until we were on the phone nearly thirty miles apart to tell me that?"

"I...umm..."

"If I was there, I'd kiss you right now," he told her. "And then I'd probably kiss you again and we'd never get our work done."

"And we have a boatload of work to do this week." She played it easy, just like him, but then he cranked it up a notch.

"But every time I look at you this week," he promised. "No matter who's in the room, or how busy you are, or how frantic things get, I want you to know that I feel exactly the same way. I'll call you later."

He hung up, wanting the last word like always, but what a last word it was. Heat bit her cheeks, and as she, Emily and Allison worked through the day, Drew's words bolstered her. And when her mother called late afternoon to say the laser ablation appeared to be a success, a huge weight lifted from the sisters' shoulders.

"But we're still retiring," Kate declared when they put her on speakerphone. "We'll talk more about that later, but Dad's already filed his retirement papers with the mayor. You girls have a crazy week ahead of you, and while Dad and I wish we could be there to help, I know everything will be just fine."

"You rest, let Dad heal and don't worry about a thing here," Emily answered. The self-assurance in her voice raised Kimberly's growing confidence in Emily's work. "This is the best present you could give us, and, oddly enough, Kimber and I make a pretty good team. Allison hasn't had to referee a fight in weeks, so that's a big step in the right direction!"

"Although I bring my whistle to work, just in case," Allison joked. "Kate, we love you guys. I'm so glad the surgery went well."

"Us, too. Gotta go. The doctors are coming in, but all is well here. Tell Rory, okay?"

"She's subbing at the elementary school for a teacher out on maternity leave, but we'll call her right now," Kimberly promised. "We love you, Mom. Give Dad a kiss for us."

"Will do!"

"What an amazing relief that is." Emily disconnected the phone, jumped up and hugged them both. "I know it doesn't come with guarantees, but I'm thrilled. I'm going to meet Rory and tell her, then I'm getting us old-fashioned fried chicken for supper, like we used to do."

"Wonderful." Kimberly meant the word sincerely. No matter what the coming weeks brought, knowing her father was doing better, being back home, welcomed into the community she had forgotten she loved… It all felt wonderful. At least until she had to tell Drew and Amy goodbye.

She couldn't think about that now. Her focus had to be on one thing this week, Shelby's wedding. For the next five days everything else went on the back-burner because this wedding wasn't just a gift for the bride. It was a gift for Drew to give to the bride and her father, reason enough to want everything perfect.

One bride. One groom. One gloriously perfect day, unmarred by anything more than the wrong shade of mascara for Shelby's close friend, and Kimberly fixed that by offering hers to the overwrought bridesmaid.

"Miss Gallagher."

"Yes, sir?" She smiled as the senator and his wife approached her once things began to quiet down midevening. She saw Drew heading their way from the opposite side of the room, and knowing the day had gone smooth as silk made her happy for the Vandeveld family, but mostly for Drew.

"We wanted to take a few moments to thank you personally," Linda told her. "I had some misgivings about the idea of barbecue at a formal affair, but I can honestly say I was pulled right back to my South Carolina roots by that food. The best I've had and the guests loved it."

"I'll pass your compliments on to Josie," she promised. "She trained with major-league chefs on the Gulf Coast, and we're blessed to have her back here."

Drew reached them at that moment. "Is everything all right?"

"Perfect," Rick declared. "We were just thanking Kimberly for all of her hard work. The entire afternoon and evening were splendid. Linda and I are beyond grateful, although I missed you on the campaign trail. I'm glad I don't have to split my defenses any longer. We're anxious to have you back, Drew."

"With the crowd of Secret Service you have at your beck and call, I'm pretty expendable now," Drew countered smoothly. "You just don't like breaking in new people, Rick, but we both know that's likely to be the reality after the election."

"I hope so," Rick agreed. "I can't say I'm not excited by the possible prospects of Pennsylvania Avenue. And, of course, you'll be with us in Washington come January. I wouldn't have it any other way." When Drew didn't answer right away, Rick studied him more intently. "Unless you're not following us to Washington."

Linda gripped his arm and shook her head slightly. "Our daughter's wedding day is not a time for business. Well, except for that envelope of checks you have for Kimberly."

"Of course." Rick reached into his pocket, withdrew a slim envelope and handed it over discreetly. "A measure of our thanks and good esteem has been included."

"Thank you." As the Vandevelds moved to say goodbye to a guest, Drew took the envelope, tucked it into his vest pocket and held out his arms. "I do believe I've been waiting for this dance, Kimber."

She'd been waiting, too, song after song, but she wasn't there to enjoy the wedding. She was there to make sure everything went according to plan. Mission accomplished.

"Do we dare?" she murmured, stepping into the circle of his arms.

"For tonight we do."

And when one arm closed around her…and her right hand was clasped in his left… It was perfect, warm and wonderful, everything she'd imagined it would be as she'd looked on all evening.

His cheek to her hair. Her head on his chest. The calm, steady beat of his heart, the kind of thing she'd love to come home to, every day.

But concern darkened Drew's eyes every time he faced Callan, and she knew Drew Slade. He couldn't be a constant source of anguish for anyone and live with himself. He'd left town once because of that. With his sacrificial heart, she had no doubt he'd do the same thing again.

"That had to be the best wedding ever!" Amy clutched the little bouquet Shelby had given her and breathed deeply late Monday afternoon. "And I never saw prettier tables! And the shiny pumpkins made everything sparkle!"

"You had fun."

Drew shot her a quick look now that everyone had left town, ready to pick up their lives where they'd left off before the big day.

"So much fun. I can't believe I was in the same room with so many famous country music people. No one will ever believe me if I tell them."

"Well, you're free to tell them now that it's over." He pulled into the drive, saw Jandro's car parked to the left of the carriage house and parked farther up the drive on purpose. "Take care of your homework and reading, okay? I've got to see what the lieutenant wants and check on Rocky."

"It looks like Nurse Mags beat you to it," Amy whispered with a finger to her lips. Her mouth formed an O, and when he saw little Mags lying next to Rocky's big kennel, he almost got choked up himself. Mags had curled up against the metal kennel, side by side with her respected adversary, and one tiny ivory paw was stretched between the bars, lying atop Rocky's huge leg in a gesture of canine love.

"I'll come down when my homework's done," she whispered.

"Okay." He crossed the front of the garage bays without waking either dog, which meant Rocky was taking his downtime seriously. "Jandro. What's up?"

"This." The lieutenant held up the letter Drew had mailed the previous week, removing his name from consideration for the police chief position. "You have everything it takes to do this job. Why are you backing out?"

He had a very good reason why. Every time Dave's son saw him, the kid was reminded of what he didn't have. A father. He didn't say that out loud, of course. Facing Jandro, he made a noncommittal face. "I realized it's not the right time. If I'd thought it through more carefully, I never would have applied."

"Well you did apply," the older officer told him bluntly. "And I'm going to pretend I didn't see this." With that, he tore Drew's letter into small, indefinable pieces and stuffed them into his pocket.

"You can't do that."

"Can. Did. Meeting is tomorrow night at the town offices at seven. Be there."

"Jandro, I—"

"Not open for discussion. If you get the job and then take the job, you can demote me for insubordination. Right now, I'm ordering you to show up at that meeting. If you leave your hometown to the likes of a guy like Brian Reynolds, shame on you."

"Hey." He tried to protest, but Jandro climbed into his car and headed down the driveway. "Jandro!"

The lieutenant ignored him, turned right and then right again, cruising down Center Street on the beautiful, crisp, autumn afternoon.

Drew kicked the curb, fuming.

How dare the lieutenant tear up his notice of withdrawal? This all could have been so simple. He'd withdraw his name, grab his kid and move on. No harm, no foul.

Except that Amy wanted to stay here. And didn't his own child deserve some kind of roots?

And leaving here meant leaving Kimberly. She'd promised her parents she'd stay and run the family business, so he couldn't even beg her to go with him and share his life somewhere else.

Corinne pulled into the driveway. Callan sat to her right, and Tee was bouncing like a crazy person in the backseat. "We wanted to check on Rocky!" she called out the back window.

"He's sleeping right now. And doing better but still dicey," Drew explained as he moved closer. "He doesn't like that he's sequestered in the kennel, but he's dealing with it."

"Aw, look at Mags." Corinne withdrew her phone and snapped a quick picture. "How sweet is that?"

"I thought she didn't like him?" Tee asked. "She was always barking at him, going crazy."

"Maybe she knows he's hurt," Callan said softly. Guilt bowed his head and rounded his shoulders as he studied Rocky in the big metal crate.

Corinne glanced from her son to the two dogs. "I think she does, Cal."

"She's showing respect for her foe," Drew told them.

"Huh? What does that mean?" Tee made a show of knotting up her face, overdramatic and crazy cute.

"Like when a runner shakes everyone's hand after a great race," Drew explained, "because they know what it took to get to that level and they respect the effort. Mags likes Rocky even though she challenges him. Like Snoopy and the Red Baron."

"I love Snoopy," Corinne said, smiling. "And we never miss a *Peanuts* special on TV."

"I remember."

Callan watched the two dogs for a moment, then stepped back. "Mom, I've got to get that book out of the library."

"Right." She grabbed Drew's arm as the kids got back into the car. "I'm glad he's doing better and that Mags has taken on nursing responsibilities. That's story-worthy, right there."

"It's funny, isn't it?" Drew glanced down at the two resting dogs. "To go from archenemies to allies like this?"

"I'd go with nice," she told him, then smiled and gave him a big hug. "Just like it's nice having you back, Drew."

She climbed into the car and pulled away a minute later. Callan turned back, watching the dogs from the back window. Remorse drew his mouth down. Worry brought his brows together.

Amy came downstairs just then. "Was Tee here?"

He nodded. "They stopped by to check on Rocky." Mags stirred when he spoke. She opened one fluff-covered eye, looked at them, then curled back into sleep alongside her big buddy.

"Was Callan with them?"

"Yes. Is he still being mean to you?" He didn't intend for the question to come out gruff, but it did, because no one should be mean to a sweet kid like Amy. Ever.

"No."

She answered quickly. Too quickly. He stared at her, one eyebrow arched, and when she blushed, a new realization swept him.

Amy had a crush on Callan. Or vice versa. Or both.

Puberty. Adolescence.

"Are we making supper or going to grab supper?" she asked, and her question changed the subject and let him off the hook.

"Let's walk to the diner and get the Monday special."

"I'd rather die," she told him, laughing. "*You* can get the meatloaf special, and I'll get chicken fingers." She grabbed his hand, and he breathed a sigh of relief. Holding his hand in public meant she was still his little girl, at least for a while.

They cut across The Square, still busy with late-day shoppers, and when they came to the Village Diner, Drew opened the door for her. A couple of folks called out their names as they made their way to a booth, and seeing Amy's answering smiles drove a point home. Amy didn't just like being *in* the town; she loved being part *of* the town. Did he have the right to jerk that out from under her, or would that be another stupid choice?

I'm coming to an intersection with too many choices...

Kimberly's words, and he understood them fully. He'd prayed over this decision, he'd shrugged it aside and then he'd prayed again.

Still no clear answer, but was that God's fault or his? Drew wasn't sure. The meeting tomorrow night would push him to choose. If all things were equal, he'd stay right where he was, in Grace Haven, with Amy and Kimberly, surrounded by old friends. But things hadn't been equal in a long time, and the thought of sacrificing Callan's happiness by his mere presence weighed heavily on his soul.

"You're not overdoing it, are you?" Kimberly scolded as her father settled himself into the passenger seat Tuesday afternoon. "Nothing can possibly be this important."

"You're wrong—it is. Now drive." His expression said he didn't appreciate getting bossed around, and Kimberly understood that because she'd inherited the trait. "Corinne and Callan are meeting us at their place."

"Okay." She dragged the word out, but did as he requested. "But I still don't know why you guys couldn't have called us, told us you were coming home. We'd have gotten things ready."

"Last-minute decision and timing was everything." She pulled into the driveway and was surprised with the ease her father handled getting out of the car.

"Dad, are you really doing as well as you seem to be?"

He flashed her a quick, endearing smile. "Yes. Praise God and the wonders of medical advances. We'll take things as they come, but yes. I'm doing well. And looking forward to retirement if Andrew Slade doesn't muck it up for me."

"Muck it up?" She frowned as she followed him in. "I don't get it."

Corinne and Callan were seated on the back porch. When Callan saw his grandfather, he raced toward them. He reached out and hugged

Kimberly's father with great care. "Grandpa! You're home!"

Pete smiled and laid an arm around the boy's shoulders. "I am, and I'm feeling better. Much better."

"Does this mean you're going to be okay?"

"It means I've got a really good shot at being okay," Pete reassured him as he hugged Corinne. "Now, there's a reason I wanted to meet with you today." His tone turned serious as he took a seat. Kimberly sat alongside him and Pete motioned for Callan to sit directly opposite him. The boy complied, curious.

"This isn't easy," Pete began.

Corinne squared her shoulders. "We're tough, Dad. We can handle whatever it is."

He met her gaze, grimaced, then shifted his attention to Callan. "I'm breaking a promise I gave years ago, and that's not something I do lightly. But this time I have no choice." He leaned forward with his hands braced on the wooden tabletop between him and his grandson. "Your dad was a great person. A great father, a great son, a great brother and a great cop. But everyone makes mistakes, son, and every now and again, those mistakes are magnified."

Callan frowned. "I don't understand."

"Your dad and Drew were friends long before they were cops. They were closer than brothers, because they loved each other when they didn't have to."

Callan's scowl deepened. "Drew had a funny way of showing it, Grandpa."

Pete ignored the comment. "The night your dad died, they'd prearranged a meet with some drug-dealing thugs, an undercover cop, Dave and Drew. Dave got there ahead of schedule, and when he thought the kingpin drug dealer was going to leave, he went in early to make the collar himself with the undercover officer."

"How do you know this?"

He turned toward Kimberly. "Because after your brother died, I read the transcripts of the call he made to Drew. Drew called him off, said he was still two minutes out. And Dave went in anyway." He turned back toward Callan as Kimberly's head swam around these new truths. "Drew wouldn't allow me to tell anyone. Ever. He took it on the chin when folks made like he let Dave down. He stood tall and strong as he helped carry your dad to the cemetery, knowing what folks thought, knowing your dad didn't follow protocol and got himself killed because of it."

"No." Callan stared at him, hard and angry. "My dad's a hero. Everyone says so."

"And I agree," Pete told him softly. "He'll always be a hero, son. But even heroes make mistakes." He stood, rounded the table and hugged his grandson. "Drew Slade is a good man. He's always been a good guy, and he sacrificed so much to ease the pain of losing David. He didn't want the last memory we had of your father to be darkened by a mistake in judgment.

"I love you, kid. You mean the world to us, but I don't want misplaced anger to get in the way of keeping Drew in Grace Haven. He's determined to leave because he thinks you hate him, and he doesn't want to be a burden to you or your mother. And that's what I came home to say."

He straightened. "There's a meeting tonight about the chief's job. I'd like to see Drew fill it, but if he thinks you blame him for his father's death, he'll likely say no. And I'd hate to see that happen." He hugged Corinne and moved toward the car. "See you later. I hope."

Kimberly exchanged looks with Corinne. "Did you have any idea?"

"None. Ever." Tears brightened Corinne's eyes. "I can see it going down just that way, though. Dave was always so brave and fearless. If he'd just waited two minutes…" Tears streamed down her face, and she sat back down. "If he was here right now, I'd smack him. Then I'd hug him and I'd never stop."

Drew hadn't been late like they'd been led to believe.

Dave had gone in early and met his fate.

God forgive me for my assumptions all those years. Forgive me for trying to blame anyone. And forgive me for not coming home sooner. Making amends.

"I've got to get Dad home. He's doing well, but I think this hit him kind of square."

"Go." Corinne reached over and hugged her son. "Cal and I will be just fine."

Kimberly didn't ask if she'd see them later. She'd promised her father she'd go to the meeting, and now she understood why. He wanted support for the changing of the guard, and with Brian's campaign for a special election, it wasn't a given. Unless Drew put the past behind him and accepted the position if it was offered.

Which is exactly what he needed to do because she'd made a promise to her parents to stay. She couldn't break her word, but she'd come to the firm conclusion that life without Drew wasn't really living. Not anymore. Which meant he had to stay as well, because being together, forming a new branch of the family, was the right thing to do.

And she had no qualms about telling him just that.

Chapter Fifteen

Drew's palms went damp as he strode into the town's meeting room Tuesday evening.

He'd keep this simple. They'd open the meeting in the traditional way, he'd stand and request his application to be withdrawn, and what could Alejandro do in front of dozens of witnesses?

Nothing.

And then he'd take a deep breath, pack up his clothes and his beautiful daughter and head back to New Jersey. He'd left Amy at the Gallaghers' on purpose, citing a possible late hour for his return. Rory had been glad to hang with her and Rocky, so his daughter would never know how close she'd come to having her dream come true.

He walked through the double doors promptly at seven o'clock, found a seat in the back of a well-filled room and sat down hard, face forward.

A moment later, someone sank into the seat

next to him. He glanced that way, and when Callan Gallagher met his gaze, his heart tightened. And when the boy stared at him, right into his eyes, then reached out and hugged him, his heart not only loosened.

It broke free.

"I'm sorry I was a jerk to you." Tears wet the boy's cheeks, and Drew wasn't sure his cheeks were any better. "Mom kept telling me it wasn't your fault, but I really just wanted it to be someone's fault that my dad died. You know?"

Drew knew, all right.

He glanced around, pretty sure Callan hadn't driven himself to the town meeting. Lined up in the back, shoulder to shoulder and hand in hand, was the entire Gallagher clan, including the ill patriarch, Pete. And Amy, too.

Pete's eyes met his. He dropped his gaze to the adolescent boy, then brought it back up to Drew, and when he tipped his chief's hat slightly, Drew knew.

Pete had intervened. He'd stepped out, broken his word to Drew and explained the truth behind Dave's death.

He'd hidden that truth a long time ago, determined to preserve Dave's integrity, professionalism and memory, but now he'd witnessed the harm and the good of shading truth. Callan's deep-seated anger showed him that.

"Ladies and gentlemen, shall we bring this meeting to order?"

They stood, recited the Pledge of Allegiance and approved the minutes. Without hesitation, the mayor announced Pete Gallagher's intended retirement. A varied chorus rounded the room, a mix of understanding and regret, but the mayor waved his hands and shushed the crowd. "We've got lots of time to get into the hoopla of the whole deal, the parties and goodbyes, everything well deserved for decades of good, honest service to our community, and we'll pay attention to all that in a few weeks. Pete's just back from some health issues, Kate's got him on a tight rope, and everyone in this room knows you don't argue with Kate Gallagher."

The crowd laughed and didn't disagree.

"Pete told me we needed to get on with the business of the day, appointing an interim police chief until Pete's elected term is up in two and a half years. And we've done that."

He looked around, spotted Drew and Callan and lifted a thin manila folder. "On behalf of the town council, the office of the mayor and the police force of Grace Haven, New York, we would like to offer the appointment of interim chief to Andrew Slade, a former city of Rochester police officer and currently the chief of security for V-Trade Incorporated and Senator Rick Vandeveld, who, as you know, is running for president."

"The senator's paying for our November festival," called out one old-timer. "That's enough to earn my vote right there."

The crowd laughed, then turned as the mayor kept his eyes locked on Drew's.

Callan took his hand on one side.

Amy came forward and took it on the other.

Trapped. In the very best possible way.

And when Kimberly moved into the seat behind him and whispered, "You're taking too long, you're out of options and you're surrounded by people who love you, including me. Just say yes, okay?"

"I accept," he told the mayor and the council. "But if the town would indulge me one more thing..." He turned, took Kimberly's hand and looked deep into her pretty blue eyes as he tried to take a knee.

The folding chair got in his way, but Callan and Amy jumped in to slide chairs left and right.

And then he took a knee properly. "Kimberly Gallagher, it just seems downright silly for both of us to be back in town and unmarried, so I propose a merger."

Her smile said she liked his unorthodox methods. "What kind of merger?"

"One where you and I get married, have a

couple more kids to drive Amy crazy and live happily ever after, no matter what happens. Because I love you, Kimber. And the only way I can do this job properly and live in the same town with you is as your husband. What do you say?"

"I say yes, Drew." She leaned down and kissed him soundly, then laughed. "I say absolutely, positively yes."

He stood and turned back toward the front and offered the mayor a quick salute. "Then it's a yes, Mayor. Draw up the paperwork, and I'll be happy to sign on."

"We're staying?" Sheer delight highlighted Amy's words. "Forever, Dad? You, me and Kimberly? This is our town?" She grabbed him in a hug, and he hugged her back, the other arm embracing his future wife.

"That's exactly what it means, darlin'." He smiled into Kimberly's eyes as he hugged Amy close, and the promise he saw there—the promise of tomorrow and every day beyond—gave him peace at last. "We've come home."

Epilogue

"Are you sure you don't mind being hurried with the wedding, Kimber?" Drew gave the posh setting of Kate & Company a quick glance the second week of November. As predicted, Rick had emerged triumphant in the elections, but Drew was now a world away. "This is your specialty. I'd understand if you want to take a little more time to plan things."

"You trying to back out of the deal, Slade?" She pushed the desk drawer shut, stood and crossed the few feet between them. "Because I have every intention of walking down the aisle of that abbey on Saturday, having Uncle Steve perform a beautiful ceremony and walking out as Mrs. Drew Slade. With a kid and a dog, so if you've got other ideas—"

"Not a one." He laughed, but he didn't laugh long because he was too busy kissing her. "I love the idea. And the idea of living together in the apartment until we close the deal on our house—"

"And the idea of having someone else help tackle the whys and wherefores of an adolescent girl."

"I won't deny how much that weighed into the decision," he joked, and when she smacked his arm, he feigned injury. "Your parents seem happy that we're doing this before they leave on their trip."

"They do, don't they?" She turned off the upstairs office lights and pulled the door shut as they walked toward the stairs down to the reception area, arm-in-arm. "It's so good to see Dad looking well, amazing, really. And no matter what happens, I'm thrilled that Emily and I can give them this time to just relax and do whatever they might want to do."

The lower door burst open. Amy and Tee raced through, saw them coming down the steps and came to a quick stop. "It's snowing!" Amy called out, clearly delighted.

"Oh, man." Drew stared at the obvious snowflakes dusting her head, then raised his gaze outside. "Snow's a fairly common occurrence up here, Amy. It gets old quick."

"Oh, it won't!" She grabbed his arm when he reached the ground floor and hugged it while she propelled him toward the door. "Look at it, Dad. So pretty, so clean and white! Isn't it beautiful?"

He looked outside.

The town lights twinkled in the freshly falling snow. Tree branches wore their dusting of white, and The Square looked as if it had been painted with the gentlest of pale brushes. "You won't mind shoveling?"

She started to answer, but Kimberly held up a hand. "We have a plowing service, so shoveling is limited to the sidewalks. Policemen and wedding planners must be able to get to work on time."

"Crucial personnel." He grinned at her, then swung open the door. A flurry of white flakes danced in the rush of air, swirling around Amy and Tee as they dashed back outside.

"Dad, I'm catching snowflakes! Try this—it's awesome!"

He didn't hesitate a moment, despite his police chief uniform and the doubtful stare Rocky shot his way.

He took his beautiful fiancée by the hand, led her into the softly falling snow and tasted snowflakes with his daughter, like he'd done as a boy more than thirty years before in the same town square.

And as the Center Street churches began their beautiful nightly chime, the blend of notes and music offered a benediction of old and new, yesterday and today, with hope for tomorrow.

And it was good.

* * * * *

Dear Reader,

I loved writing this story for many reasons. Years ago a wonderful family offered me a job as a bridal consultant in their store. That opportunity laid the groundwork for long-lasting friendships and the basis for delightfully fun bridal books. I am truly blessed!

But mostly this book is dedicated to the officers lost in the line of service. Our church was hit hard by this several years ago when a wonderful young trooper was gunned down during a routine traffic stop. In 2014, 134 American lawmen and women were killed in the line of duty. I am honoring them in this series by using their first names for all of the male characters. My respect for law and order runs deep, and the loss of lives casts a ripple effect on so many.

I hope you love this story like I do, and I love to hear from readers! E-mail me at loganherne@gmail.com, visit me at ruthloganherne.com or friend me on Facebook where I love to chat, laugh and pray! You can also reach me by snail mail c/o Love Inspired Books, 233 Broadway, Suite 1001, New York, NY 10279.

Thank you so much for choosing *An Unexpected Groom*, and I look forward to hearing from you!

Ruthy

MONTANA
MAVERICKS